All the

Poses

A Pretty Series Novel

By

M. LEIGHTON

There is no fear in love.
1 John 4:18

Being deeply loved by someone gives you strength, while loving
someone deeply gives you courage.
Lao Tzu

To Courtney
You are the most amazing friend and crit partner a girl could ask
for. I love you to the moon!

To Autumn, Kathryn and Megan
Thank you from the bottom of my heart. I feel like you three
helped me make this book shine. I adore you all!

CHAPTER ONE

REESE

"Hot dayum! This is awesome!" Sig Locke says when I lead our little party through the doors of *Exotique*, one of several high-end dance clubs that I own.

"Are you sure you want to do this?" Hemi, my younger brother, is speaking to his girlfriend, Sloane.

She smiles up into his face. "Babe, this is for Sig. I want to make his first trip to Chicago a memorable one. I already told you that. Besides," she says, leaning up to bite his chin, "maybe I can learn some moves."

Hemi's smile is slow, but I know what he's thinking. He's already picturing her working a pole in a private show that's just for him.

"Oh, God!" Sig says, covering his ears with his hands. "I do *not* need to hear this shit!"

I chuckle and shake my head, stopping for a second to look around.

I'm always filled with a mixture of pride and arousal when I walk into one of my clubs. I've built an empire of very classy, very high-end exotic dance clubs that spans the United States and several other countries. And although I don't get to visit all of them more than once or twice a year at most, I always get a charge out of walking into one.

Everything is exactly as I left it when I was here thirteen months ago. The black marble floors are buffed to a shine, the chrome bar sits under a bank of soft overhead lights and all the gorgeous cocktail waitresses are dressed in sleeveless, tuxedo dresses that bear a shitload of cleavage and stop at the top of their thighs. Classy. Sexy. Mine.

I know I could walk up to any one of them and, within ten minutes, leave with them. I wouldn't even have to tell them who I am. It's just one of the many gifts I possess. I'm not arrogant about it. It's just fact. I have something they want. And *they* have something *I* want. For the night anyway.

But now's not the time for that. Tonight, I'm here for my little brother, Hemi. I told him he and his girlfriend, Sloane could sail with me on one of my luxury yachts to Hawaii where we'd drop them off for a two-week vacation that I've arranged for them. Her brother was a surprise, but… whatever. It's the least I could do for Hemi since he found and brought to justice the dirty cop whose actions led to the death of our youngest brother, Ollie.

"Come on," I tell our group, "this way."

When Hemi told me they wanted to come out here tonight, I called and had the manager hold open one of the VIP seating areas for us. It sits slightly to the left of the stage, close enough to smell the dancers' perfume. If my brother's innocent little girlfriend wants to learn some moves, I'll give her the best seat in the house.

I recognize a few of the girls we pass. I'm surprised they're still here. I don't remember their names, but I *do* remember something distinct about each one.

Blonde waitress—screamer.

Red-headed bartender—likes it rough.

Another blonde waitress—clingy. Seeing her glare at me as I walk by reminds me of how unpleasant things got when she finally realized that I meant what I said. *Don't get attached. I'm not interested in a relationship.*

She found out the hard way.

Once we're seated, a nice-looking brunette with mile-long legs and tits that sit up under her chin comes to take our order. The smile she gives me is very... interested. Whether she knows who I am or not, I'd bet anybody a thousand dollars I could get her to sneak into the bathroom with me. Something quick and hot. Something meaningless. But with my current company, I can't really do anything like that tonight.

Pity, I think as I appraise her surgically-enhanced figure once more.

"I'm sorry, what did you say your name was again? Or should I just call you 'mine'?" I tease with a wink.

I'm not surprised by the reaction I get. She leans down closer to me, giving me a bird's eye view of her assets, and whispers huskily, "Pandora, but you can call me anything you want, *including* yours."

I arch my brow and give her a half smile. "How about we start with a round of shots first? Patron. On me. Start a tab. Keep 'em coming."

Her eyes are gleaming with attraction. I know it when I see it. I've seen it *a lot.* "And your name, sir?" she asks, her tongue sneaking out to wet one corner of her full lips.

"Reese Spencer."

Her eyes round almost imperceptibly.

Almost.

She knows who I am. It's not easy to find out that I own this club, but word gets around occasionally. And word must've gotten around to her.

"Yes, sir. I'll be right back with those shots."

I nod my thanks and turn my attention to the stage as the house lights dim and the spotlight flicks on. The music changes and all eyes turn to see the gorgeous platinum blonde strut out onto the T-shaped runway that leads from the back and the dressing rooms to the stage.

I watch with muted enthusiasm. I enjoy watching the dancers and I'm glad the club is running smoothly and that things are in order, but more than anything, I just want the night to be over so that I can go and get some rest before tomorrow. I have a funeral to attend.

I drink while my brother and his girlfriend tease each other. I would find their easy love enviable, if I cared anything about having that kind of relationship. But I don't, so I barely pay them any attention.

I look away from them, ignoring their gushing and public displays of affection in favor of Sloane's older brother, Sig. He seems to be a pretty nice guy, and he's enjoying the hell out of my club.

"Good god! She needs to bring that ass right down here and sit it in my lap," he says when another pretty blonde with more pronounced curves comes out onto the stage.

He laughs and howls, throwing back another shot and chasing it with his Southern Comfort and Sprite. He catches me eyeing him and howls even louder, giving me a playful punch in the arm.

"Drink up, man! I need somebody to get drunk with. Something about being at a club like this with my sister is flipping my shit!" He laughs a little harder than what is probably warranted.

"I think you're doing just fine on your own," I tell him, making note of it when he loses his balance and nearly falls out of his chair.

I'm thinking of making my excuses and leaving when the music changes yet again, stopping me. The sexy thump of Madonna's *Justify My Love* strikes me as an interesting yet odd choice for a dance, and it draws my attention back to the platform.

From the left side of back stage, a girl emerges. She walks slowly along the runway. The spotlight follows her and I see that she's wearing a man's dress shirt and tie. And nothing else.

Her legs are long—with the stilettos she's wearing, even longer—and perfectly toned. Dancer's legs. Strong. Graceful. Sinful.

Each step she takes is a sexy, sensual movement of them. Slow. Deliberate. I sit up a little straighter in my seat. I'm immediately catapulted from mildly interested to extremely intrigued and I don't really know why. I've seen hundreds of dancers do hundreds of dances. But I've never seen *this one*. And something about *this one* has all my senses on point.

As she draws closer, I can see that her rich brown hair is covered by a hat that sits at a cocky angle on her head. In her hand is a shiny black cane. When she gets to center stage, she stops, swinging the cane once before propping it out in front of her body. In one excruciatingly measured movement, she stiffens her legs and bends forward, showing off the length of her perfect thighs as they ease into the curve of her perfect ass.

Before I'm finished looking, she straightens, twirling the cane up over her head and taking one end in each hand. She arches her back, forcing what looks like some luscious tits up and out. Then, still moving slowly, she eases the cane down the front of her body.

Each action is smooth and unhurried. Each movement is sexy and fluid, her body melting from one into the next in perfect time to the music.

I glance up at her face. Beneath the shadow of her hat, all I can see is her mouth. But damn, what a mouth it is! Her lips are painted bright red and are probably the lushest ones I've ever seen. They're what I've always called dick-sucking lips—plump, pouty and perfectly formed to slip down over the head of my cock.

Not having been overly enthused about coming tonight *or* about the entertainment, I'm surprised that my dick twitches when she pulls her lower lip between her teeth and bites down. But damn if it doesn't.

I feel a groan build in my chest when she drops slowly to her knees, sliding the cane away from her body like she's doing a push-up, slinking down onto her stomach. After a few beats, she abandons the cane and eases over onto her back, her hips turning last, like a cat that's getting ready to stretch. I can almost feel the purr.

Legs flat on the stage, she runs her hands from the tops of her thighs to her stomach, pulling the hem of her shirt up just enough to give a teasing glimpse of what she's wearing underneath before moving on to her breasts and throat. Her nimble fingers work loose the tie, dragging it slowly from around her neck. Purposefully, she twists her hands, winding the silk around her wrists.

For a few seconds, it's just me and this girl. Alone in this room. With nothing between us but this music. And that damned tie. All too clearly, images of me tying her up with that scrap of red material flit through my mind, making me throb behind my zipper.

Languorously, she stretches one leg straight up into the air, the other lying flat on the stage. She reaches up and grabs her ankle, skimming her bound hands to her knee, pulling that leg toward her face. Her thighs widen into a perfect split that reveals little black, satin panties. When I see them, all I can think about is kneeling between those legs and kissing that silky material.

I see her lips pucker as she puts one chaste kiss on her knee. I'm enthralled. But it's when I see her tongue flicker out that I feel like I could punch a hole through the bottom of the table with my hard-on. There's something about her that's so understatedly sexy. It's like she doesn't even know we're here, like she's lost inside her own head. And God, how I'd love to be part of what she's imagining!

I feel a hand on my arm, interrupting the scene. I'm instantly aggravated by the intrusion. I jerk away, not even bothering to turn around until I hear a voice.

It's my brother. And he's determined to get my attention. Finally, I turn, not even trying to hide my agitated glare.

"What?"

"Can you take us back home? Sloane's not feeling well. Something she ate earlier maybe." He gives me a meaningful look. It takes me a second to fully disengage from the girl that had me so rapt, but eventually (reluctantly) I do. And I remember that Sloane didn't drink her shot of tequila. Then I remember why. Hemi told me she's pregnant, but that they haven't told her family yet, so he asked me not to say anything.

"Oh...right," I respond a bit too sharply. "Yeah, I can take you."

Hesitant to leave just yet, I glance back toward the front of the room in time to see that the dancer is on her knees again, throwing off her hat. A mane of silky chestnut curls falls down. I only get a brief flash of her face. Her hair swirls around to obscure her features. But not before I get a glimpse of one pale green eye. And the way it widens when it meets mine.

Instantly, I'm transported back in time. Years and years ago. To the soft grass of a clearing in the woods. And the smooth skin of the girl beneath me.

I remember those eyes. That mouth. I remember a slightly ganglier, less mature version of this woman's body. How it felt to touch her, to hold her. How she laughed, how she tasted. How it ended.

And how I could never forget.

Holy god!

It's Kennedy.

CHAPTER TWO

KENNEDY

My heart slams to a stop in my chest and I forget to breathe when my eyes collide with the luminous blue-green ones that I've never been able to completely put behind me.

Reese.

As he stands before me, I take him in. Within a fraction of a second, I catalog his every feature.

He's aged beautifully. He's still the same tall, ungodly handsome guy that he was all those years ago, but now he's a man. A breathtaking man.

His shoulders seem wider, if that's possible. Stronger. His arms are long and powerful in his dress shirt, his biceps straining against the expensive material, even in rest. His waist is trim, his stomach flat and his thighs are as thick as ever. It's what lies between them that brings color to my cheeks—the impressive bulge behind his zipper.

As much as I've struggled to put that day out of my mind, it all rushes back with crystalline clarity. I remember what it felt like to be pierced by him, both emotionally and physically. And I remember what it felt like to be crushed by him, too.

He's standing perfectly still, watching me. Recognizing me. As his eyes travel my body, I feel them as though he is touching me. Again. Like before.

I feel the pressure of his kiss when the aqua orbs stop on my lips. I feel the tickle of them as his gaze skates down my throat to where my chest is heaving beneath my costume shirt. When his perusal stops on my breasts, my nipples tingle with the remembered feel of his palms against them. And when he moves on to my stomach, stopping at the short hem of my shirt where it barely covers my black panties, I feel a gush of unwanted heat.

Unwanted because I stopped wanting Reese years ago. Stopped loving him. I had to. To survive.

And then his eyes rise to mine again. In them, I see recognition, a little anger, a little more desire and shock. A lot of shock.

All this transpires in a few short heartbeats. When I drag my eyes away, I realize that I'm shaking. I struggle to maintain my composure for the few remaining seconds of the song. When my number draws to an end, I make myself take slow, measured steps as I turn to walk away. But it's not easy. In fact, it's the second hardest thing I've ever had to do in my life.

CHAPTER THREE

REESE

It takes my brother slapping the back of my shoulder to get my eyes off of Kennedy as she walks away.

"You coming?"

Five minutes ago, I couldn't wait to get home, but now...now, all I really want to do is go back stage and find Kennedy. I have no idea what I'd do after that. Kiss her. Shake her. Ask her what in the ten rings of hell she's doing dancing in one of my clubs. But I can't.

Well, I *could*, but I won't. I *shouldn't*.

Suddenly, I feel angry. And frustrated.

"Reese, man, what the hell?" Hemi prompts.

"I'm coming," I snap, turning away from the stage so fast that my chair tips over. I nearly run right into our waitress, on her way back to our table with Sig's next shot and my next drink.

She gasps in surprise. "I'm sorry. Pardon me."

"My fault," I tell her, grabbing her arm to keep her from stumbling backward.

She leans into me, looking up at me with her big blue eyes. "Thank you," she breathes, her breasts brushing my chest.

My first thought is that her eyes are the wrong color; they should be sea foam green. My second thought is a string of long, very harsh obscenities. My third thought is that maybe this girl is *exactly* what I need tonight after all.

"What time do you get off?"

"That all depends on you," she replies suggestively. Unfortunately for her, my mood has changed. Drastically.

"Just give me the keys, Reese. We'll wait in the car," Hemi says from my left, blatantly annoyed. Unfortunately for *him,* he just gave me the window that I needed.

I take the keys to my Mercedes out of my pocket and slap them into his palm. "I'll be out in ten."

As soon as Hemi's girlfriend is on her feet, with her back toward me, I tug my "distraction" in closer to my chest as I whisper down into her ear, "How do you feel about the men's room?"

"Tonight, it's my favorite place," she purrs.

"That's what I thought."

And just like that, Kennedy is off my mind.

I lead Pandora to the men's room, making sure it's empty before I lock the door and pull her into my arms. She comes willingly. Like I knew she would.

I grab her ass in one hand and one plump tit in the other, squeezing both as I drag my lips over her throat.

"Tell me what you like," she moans, swiveling her hips in just such a way that she massages my throbbing cock.

"I wanna see you playing with these," I tell her, spreading the lapels of her top and baring her naked breasts, "while you're blowing me with these." I cover her lips with my own, sucking the lower one into my mouth and biting it with my teeth.

As soon as I release her, the hot brunette kisses and rubs her way down my neck and chest, then on to my stomach before I feel her cup my balls through my pants. I groan, leaning my head back against the cool tile wall as she unzips my pants and dips her hand inside.

The first touch of her tongue to the tip of my cock draws a groan from me. She licks and sucks, trailing her lips along the length from base to tip, but it's not enough. I need…more. I need to bang something— or someone—*hard*. The waitress's mouth slides down over my shaft, taking as many inches as she can all the way down into her throat. By touch, I reach down to thread my fingers into her hair, guiding her over me. Harder and harder, faster and faster.

My mistake is in raising my head to look down at her. She pauses to glance up and all I can see is that it's the wrong eyes. The wrong mouth. The wrong face.

The wrong woman.

And just like that, Kennedy is on my mind again. Under my skin.

With an angry growl, I pull my dick out of the waitress's mouth.

"What's wrong, baby?" she asks in a pouty, sexy voice, a voice that merely grates on my nerves at this point.

"Nothing you can fix. It's not you, it's... it's just... Maybe you should just go back to work," I tell her as pleasantly as I can, zipping up my pants and moving away from her. I'm so frustrated, all I want to do is put my fist through the wall. And then put my cock into Kennedy.

Angrily, I turn toward the sink to wash my hands. In the mirror, I don't see the muted fury of the eyes that are staring back at me. No, I see blatant disgust in the pale green ones that I've never been able to forget.

With a shake of my head, I look back and see only *my* reflection and, behind me, the waitress. Kennedy is nowhere to be found.

Except in my head.

Where she never left.

CHAPTER FOUR

KENNEDY

My heart is still hammering when I ease into the chair in front of my dressing table back stage. I glance down at my hands. They're shaking.

Reese Spencer.

"What the hell's the matter with you?" I glance over at Karmen, the resident Southern Belle right here in Chicago, where she's brushing the long, black wig that she'll wear for her next dance. "You look like you just saw a ghost."

My laugh is dry. "Yeah, that's pretty much what happened."

"Tell mama all about it," she coos as she drags the brush through the silky strands. When I send her a wry look, she winks at me. "No, seriously. Tell me what happened. This is the most worked up I've seen you since you started here."

I don't normally share *any* of my business with the other girls. I'm a very private person. Always have been. Sometimes out of necessity, sometimes out of choice, but always private. That's why I'm a little surprised when my mouth opens up and half my life story falls out.

"I just saw someone that I haven't seen in years. I knew him when I was younger. I thought he was...he was...wow! I mean, he was just..." I pause and sigh. "It was like *that*," I say, raising my brows meaningfully. "I thought the sun rose and set in his eyes." In fact, I can remember watching a sunrise in his fathomless aqua eyes. Once. Before... I feel the pang of remembered devastation tug at my heart, like fresh new skin pulling at an old scar. "But then he left and never came back. I haven't seen him since. Until tonight."

I'm lost in thought, in memory, for what feels like an eternity before I realize that neither Karmen nor I have said another word. I shake my head to clear it and give her what I hope is a bright smile. "It was a long time ago."

Karmen's expression is pensive. And *her mind* is perceptive. "You loved him," she observes.

My mouth opens to deny it, but the words don't come out. It's almost like my body won't let me breathe such a betrayal, one that would minimize the pure hell I went through after he left. Yes, I loved him. With my entire soul, I loved him. And he left me. Just like that.

"As much as a young, naïve girl can love a guy like that, I suppose," I reply, matter of fact.

"A guy like what?"

"Rich. Handsome. Privileged. Heartless."

"Honey, guys like that are the easiest ones *to* love. Something in us wants to be the one to tame them, to be the one they change for. Maybe. Hell, I don't know. I just know they're the ones that are the most dangerous. From what I hear, our dear Pandora found that out for herself tonight."

Still firmly road-blocked on memory lane, I'm barely paying attention to what she's saying about Pandora. "Hmmm. And why is that?"

"She thought she'd snag her one of the big fish. According to her, she had a 'run-in' with the owner of the club, out in the men's room. She found out the hard way, though, that guys like that *are* the way *they are* for a reason."

I frown. "The owner?"

"Yeah. He doesn't come here very often. I've only seen him one other time. But when he does come, he always makes a stir. Of course, a guy like that makes a stir *wherever* he goes. I mean, he *is* hot as Georgia in July, but men like him don't change. Ever. For anyone."

"She's better off. He sounds like a beast. I mean, the bathroom for god's sake?" I shake my head in disgust.

Karmen grins. "Oh, she wasn't complaining about that part. She was just hoping for more. A guy like that makes *all the girls* hope."

"Surely she's making that up. I just don't understand how something like that even happens. I mean, she was *working!*"

She shrugs one delicate shoulder. "Pandora takes 'serving' the VIP section to a whole new level." Karmen laughs at her cleverness.

I sit up a little straighter in my chair, a terrible sinking sensation invading the pit of my stomach. "VIP section? Which table was this guy at?"

There's only one man I know—only one man I've *ever* known—who can command this kind of attention. He commanded mine fourteen years ago. And he commanded it again tonight, even after nearly ruining my life.

"Two. You didn't see him?"

Table two. The section where Reese was sitting. Although I'd like to think Karmen is talking about someone else, I know in my gut that she's not.

"Yeah, I think I did."

I close my eyes. I refuse—*refuse*—to give Reese Spencer one more ounce of heartache, one more millisecond of pain, one more drop of tears. I gave him enough fourteen years ago.

CHAPTER FIVE

REESE

I'm grouchy as hell. Even *less* in the mood for my uncle's funeral than I was last night.

I woke up with a raging hard-on. The same one I went to bed with. The one that I got from seeing Kennedy up on that stage. The one that the hot waitress who could suck a golf ball through a garden hose couldn't get rid of last night in the bathroom. *That* hard-on.

Needless to say, I'm not looking forward to seeing my father. He'll be attending, partially out of respect but mostly because of public perception. *I'll* be attending because I loved my uncle. Probably more than I love my father, which is sad. Sad, but true.

The funeral is being held at Bellano, the home of my ancestors that lies in the outskirts of Chicago. It's one of the few remaining undisturbed tracts of land. It's worth a bloody fortune, but it will never be sold. As the eldest, my uncle inherited it and, today, we will learn who will be responsible for keeping it in the family through the next generation. I'm guessing it will be my father since Malcolm had no children.

I notice that the sparse trees that line the road leading to Bellano begin to thicken. It's the first indication that the estate is close. Few trees turn into several, and several into many, until the road is nothing more than a thin line of asphalt cut into dense forest.

Up ahead, I see the gap in the vegetation and I press the brake to slow the car. I make a right turn and ease up to the wide wrought iron gates. The two halves that form an intricate S in the middle when closed now stand open, welcoming mourners to the site of Malcolm Spencer's funeral.

I drive slowly along the winding path that leads to the main house. I spent many a summer here. Happy summers. Some of the best times of my life. Until my father put an end to it by sending me to college at Oxford.

As I begin up a slight incline, the main house comes into view. To most it looks imposing, what with its gray stone exterior and multiple turrets, but to me, it's warm and inviting. Because my uncle lived here. And he was always good to me.

I park in the spot I used during my summer visits — to the left of the five-car garage, in the grassy space between it and the side entrance to the kitchen. When I cut the engine, I sit in the quiet for a few minutes, remembering all the times I pulled up in just such a way. I glance up at the kitchen window, half expecting Tanny, my uncle's housekeeper, to be there watching for me, just like she always was. Today, however, the kitchen window is empty. My uncle is dead. And I'm sure Tanny got tired of waiting for me to come back.

I'm a little surprised at the pang of guilt I feel at the notion. I've spent the last dozen or so years perfecting the art of never being wrong and never feeling guilty. In a way, both of those are as much a mindset as they are a fact. At least to Spencer men they are. And Spencer men are never wrong. Which means we never have to feel guilty.

Until today. When I'm making my first trip back to Bellano in over a decade. I never came back. Because my father raised the perfect replica of a perfect bastard.

Me.

Swallowing the heavy feeling that something is lodged in my throat, I get out and make my way to the front door. I button my jacket as I walk through the foyer, noting that it smells exactly as it had the last time I was here—like pipe smoke. My uncle loved his pipe. And somehow, it suited him. Even the tobacco he favored suited him. It was a rich, warm scent. Homey. Welcoming. Much like him.

He was nothing like my father. Thank God.

Two ushers, dressed in black suits and crisp white shirts, are manning the door leading into the library, my uncle's favorite room. It's fitting that he'd want the service held here where mourners could visit him for the last time in the place he loved most.

As soon as I enter the room, my eyes fall on my father where he stands near the door, his arms crossed disapprovingly over his chest.

"What are you doing here?" he asks.

I keep my eyes riveted to his, a habit I formed long ago. No matter what else is going on, always maintain eye contact. With a man like Henslow Spencer, looking away is a sign of weakness. And you never want to let him think you're weak. Or that you're backing down.

"Have you forgotten how much time I used to spend here with Uncle Malcolm?"

The disgusted curl of my father's upper lip is reflected in the cold glint of his steely blue eyes. "No, I haven't forgotten. I haven't forgotten how you used to run here like a little coward and how he used to indulge your silly fantasies. No, I haven't forgotten how much time you spent with my brother. But I *had* thought that maybe you'd learned better judgment since you were that foolish boy."

"Better judgment?" I ask, biting my tongue and keeping to myself all the other things I'd like to say. I would never disrespect my uncle by making a scene at his viewing.

"Yes, than to come back *here,*" he sneers, his disdain for Bellano clear. He stopped thinking of it as his home place the day Malcolm moved back in.

"Not all of us hated it here," I tell him, forcing my lips into a tight smile so that no one else can see the strain between us.

"Not all of us were ignorant children."

With great effort, I hold my smile in place, nodding formally to him before I give him my polite response. "If you'll excuse me, I'd like to go pay my respects."

I don't give him a chance to answer. I simply continue on my way as though he never stopped me.

I make my way to the front of the room, to the coffin. I feel a pang of regret that there's no one standing in a receiving line in front of it. My uncle was a widower with no children. It was just him and Tanny. And me. Until I left him all those years ago.

As always when I think of it, bitterness burns in my gut. Bitterness toward my controlling father who took advantage of the impressionable boy he could push around. I only wish I'd grown my iron backbone a few years sooner. Maybe my uncle wouldn't have died alone.

A vase full of roses sits on a small, round table at the end of the coffin stand. I take one and walk to my uncle's side, laying the rose upon his chest alongside the few others. He loved roses. For years after his wife, my aunt Mary, died, he kept up her rose garden, made sure that it flourished when nothing else did. I'm sure the roses here came from that garden. He'd have wanted nothing less.

As I withdraw my hand, my fingers brush his. They're cold and stiff. Lifeless. Like my uncle is now. I glance up at his still face, the angles and planes of it so familiar to me, so much like my father's. Only softer. Less rigid. Much like Malcolm. He was the "human" Spencer brother. My father...wasn't.

Still isn't.

I feel a gentle hand in the center of my back. I see a slight woman with short, light brown hair appear at my left. It's Mrs. Tannenbaum, my uncle's housekeeper and his only real companion since Mary died. She raises watery, soft blue eyes to mine and does her best to smile. As it is, it's not much more than a shaky spread of the alabaster skin around her mouth.

I bend to hug her delicate frame. The feel of her arms coming around me is immediately comforting. Just like it always was, all those years ago. "Tanny."

"Harrison," she replies warmly, squeezing me. When she leans back, she reaches up to cup my cheek and pat it gently. "I'm so glad you came." Tears fill her eyes and I feel another pang of guilt.

"Of course I came." Her smile says she wasn't so sure I would, which makes me feel even worse. I clear my throat. "How are you?"

"I'm hanging in there. How are you?"

"I'm well," I say, examining her face. While she's an attractive older woman with her perfectly coiffed hair and cornflower blue eyes, she seems to have aged a hundred years since last I saw her. I knew Malcolm's death would be hard for her.

"It's been so long. And it's so good to see you," she declares, her expression flooded with sincerity. "Malcolm and I missed you so much around here. How have you been? Have you put on weight?" she asks, backing up to assess me.

I can't help but grin. "Since I was nineteen? I'm sure I've gained a pound or two."

"You needed to. You were so thin back then."

"I wasn't *that* thin, Tanny. I was just active."

"Well, you look healthy and hale now. I'm glad to see you're eating well. And still so handsome. Have you married yet?"

"No, still not married."

She rubs my arm and winks as if to reassure me. "Don't you worry about that, my sweet. The right girl is out there somewhere. Don't rush it. Just wait for her."

"Oh, I'm not rushing anything," I tell her honestly.

"Good. *Some* mistakes can haunt you for the rest of your life."

Something in her eyes tells me she has some personal experience with ghosts, but I have no idea what they might be. It occurs to me that, as well as I know Tanny, I don't really know her at all. I make a silent resolution right here and now to visit her more often. Provided that she still has a job when all is said and done.

The thought of my father firing her when he takes over the house makes my insides roil with rage. But, for Tanny, I hide my anger behind a pleasant smile.

"I do my best not to make mistakes."

Tanny's expression falls into one of mild disapproval. "That sounds like something your father would say."

I don't have a chance to respond before Tanny sees someone over my shoulder and her face lights up again.

"Oh, it's my beautiful girl," she says, moving past me, arms spread in preparation for another hug.

I turn, ready with a pleasant smile, but it's wiped from my face the instant I see who Tanny is hugging.

It's Kennedy.

Today, she looks more like what I remember, like what I would've expected to see, even after all these years. Her chestnut hair hangs in a smooth, gleaming sheet to the middle of her back, her face is bare of makeup because she really doesn't need it, and her slender body is concealed beneath a plain black dress that falls to just below the knee.

But none of that can rid my mind of the way she looked last night.

A series of emotions flood me, desire first and foremost. Now I have memories of her seductive dance to add to those from my youth, ones of tasting her sweet skin on a bed of soft grass in the forest no more than a few hundred yards from where I'm standing. The other emotions are secondary, but no less potent.

Frustration because, still, I would like nothing more than to sink between those long, long legs and lose myself for at least a day. Anger because she is far too innocent to be dancing at one of *my* clubs the way she was. More frustration because I loved it. And more anger because other men got to see it.

It's that anger that propels me forward. "Well, well, well, if it isn't the tiny dancer." My tone is cold and bitter even to my own ears. Just like my father's.

Kennedy straightens from Tanny's arms, her expression stung, her cheeks pink. She tucks her chin and glances left and right, as though she's checking to see if anyone else is listening. Finally, she returns her attention to me. Her smile is tight, but polite.

"Reese, it's been a long time."

"Yes, it has. Seems like a lot has changed since I left."

Her smile falters. "That happens when people leave without a word and don't come back for almost two decades," she grinds out from between her gritted teeth.

I deserved that, but I'm not in the habit of being derailed by something as simple as guilt. That's one reason I decided to stop feeling it. It's a weak feeling for weak people.

The perfect clone of the perfect bastard, I think for a moment before I push the thought aside and return to my anger.

"I don't have time for this," I snap, stepping forward to take Kennedy by the arm and tug her along with me as I stride across the room to the door that leads to the conservatory just off the library.

"What the hell is the matter with you?" Kennedy hisses when the door shuts behind us and we are out of view of the people in the library. She wrenches her arm free.

"I'm the one asking questions. Now would you like to tell me what you are doing dancing in one of my clubs?"

She raises her chin defiantly. "I didn't know it was *your club* until last night when you accosted one of the waitresses in the men's room. Word got around pretty fast after that," she spits in disgust.

I grind my back teeth together. I don't know why I care that she knows about that. Even though she did little more than lick my dick before I stopped her, it still pisses me off. "Don't change the subject. Why are you dancing in a place like that?"

Kennedy narrows her eyes on me. "What's the matter? Feeling a little ashamed of the type of businessman you've become, Reese?"

"I'm not ashamed of anything. My clubs are some of the best in the world. They're just no place for a girl like you."

"And what's that supposed to mean? Just what kind of girl am I?"

"You *used* to be a nice one."

"Just because I do what I love in a club like yours doesn't mean I'm not a nice girl. It's not a strip club, for god's sake."

"It's still not a place for someone like you."

Kennedy's laugh is bitter and so is her expression. "I hate to break it to you, Reese, but most of the world has to work for a living. And, just in case you didn't realize it, your clubs pay very, very well."

I stare at her and she stares at me. I want to yell until she hears me, to grab her and make her promise she won't ever return there, but I also am suddenly overcome with the desire to help her. She's just working a job to pay the bills, like ninety-nine percent of the population. But knowing that she's forced to dance for the pleasure of men hits me in a soft place that I didn't even realize I had.

"Then let me get you a job in the administrative offices. There are dozens of other positions I could put you in with the company."

"I'm sure that's your way of trying to be nice, but I don't need your charity, Reese. I've done just fine on my own all this time. Besides, dancing is what I love. It's what I've always wanted to do. Your club is just a stepping stone. Trust me, *Reese,* I have dreams far beyond dancing in *your club.*"

"And what are those?"

"Why do you care?"

"I don't know. Maybe I just do."

A frown wrinkles Kennedy's brow. Her sea foam eyes search mine as though she's discerning whether or not I'm genuinely interested or if there's a trap somewhere ahead.

"You really want to know?"

"I do." And that's no lie. Just as when we were kids, I find that I'm unusually interested in Kennedy.

"Ultimately, I'd love to dance with an amazing troupe like Altman American Dance Theater. But since that's not very likely, I'd settle for small theater dance. My dream is just to dance. *Really* dance."

Her voice is quiet. Sincere.

And for reasons I'll never know, I do something incredibly stupid.

"Come work the summer for me, then. On my boat. Then I'll get you an audition with Chance Altman."

CHAPTER SIX

KENNEDY

"What? A-are you serious?" I stutter.

"Deadly," Reese replies flatly.

"Work for you. Doing what?"

One dark brow arches suggestively, sending a little shiver through me, but then it falls back down before he answers. "Nothing you haven't done before." When I open my mouth to take exception to such a vague description, he continues. "Some dancing, socializing. Maybe serving some drinks. Nothing too taxing."

"And for that, you'll get me an audition. With Altman. How?"

"Very easily. I've had the pleasure of Chance's company on one of my boats before. As well as in a few of my clubs. Let's just say he owes me."

"I just...I can't...And all I'd have to do is work for you. On a boat. For the summer."

Reese smiles. That smile that turned my world upside down. And then left it in a smoldering heap of burned ruin.

I am so overcome with emotion right now, I'm finding it hard to keep a grip on rational thought.

Seeing Reese last night was like a bullet to the heart. Feeling those aqua eyes on me brought back everything in one mind-numbing rush.

The draw, like gravity.

The desire, like obsession.

The pain, like annihilation.

I thought I was over him. For years, I've thought I was over him, but seeing him again...even for three minutes...right out of the blue...God, it was like being hit by a car going ninety miles an hour. All over again. The instant I saw him, everything I ever felt for him came crashing back down on me, like an avalanche. One that it took me half my life to crawl out from under.

But then, finding out what he did with Pandora just a few minutes after our eyes locked... it was like losing him all over again. The disappointment was devastating. I spent the night holding back tears, both old and new, reminding myself that I left Reese behind a long, long time ago. As I finally drifted off to sleep, I kept reminding myself that I have to leave him in my past, not let him touch my *now* in the tiniest way.

Yet here I am, listening to his proposition, actually considering it, because he's dangling the *one* carrot that could make me question whether or not I should turn around and walk away. For good. Forever.

"What if I'm married? Did you ever think of that?"

For the blink of an eye, I see his nostrils flare in anger, but then Reese surprises me by giving me a half-grin, his sparkling eyes intense as they shine down into mine.

"You're not married."

"And how do you know that?"

"Because if you were mine, I would never, *ever* let you dance like that." Reese takes another step closer to me, reaching up to touch my cheek with the very tip of one finger. "Unless it was just for me."

I'm breathless. I shouldn't be. But I am. "Maybe he just likes to watch me dance," I say, struggling to keep from falling under the spell of his closeness.

"I wouldn't blame him. *I* loved watching you. But I didn't love *everyone else* watching you."

Reese's eyes flicker down to my mouth, making my lips tingle again. I'm stuck in some surreal place between what *was* and what *is*. Some part of me is teetering on the edge of the ocean of passion and desire that Reese and I once drifted within. But another part of me, the scarred part, remembers what it felt like to drown in those waters.

Helpless. And all alone.

I take a step back. "Well I guess it's a good thing I'm not yours then, right, Reese?"

"But you could be," he says softly, not moving any closer, eyes just as intense.

My heart is aching in my chest. The girl in me, the one who loved him so deeply so many years ago, wants to run to him, to throw myself in his arms and ask him where he's been all this time. But the woman in me, the woman who had to clean up the mess of that girl, the one who suffers the echoes of all those tears, knows that there is nothing to run back to. There never was.

"Is that what this is about? You getting another shot at little Kennedy?" I can't keep the bitterness from my tone, so I don't even try. "Because I'm not that little girl anymore."

"Oh, I can see that."

"I won't retrace her footsteps, Reese. You should know that now. If you make this offer, and if I accept, it'll be strictly professional."

Reese sighs. "I want to help you, Kennedy. I really do. And I will. But I won't deny that I *want* you." He takes one easy step toward me. "Or that I intend to have you."

My insides quake. His words...the memories...that look in his eyes...

But I reach down deep for the strong Kennedy that rose from the ashes of the girl that knelt at Reese's feet. I wrap myself in her confidence, in her resolve. It's *her* that gives Reese my most stunning smile. "Then I hope you're okay with disappointment, because there's no way in hell I'd go down that road again."

Reese nods his head regally, a silent *Touché*. It's as I turn to walk away that he lands his parting shot.

"Just don't expect me to help you resist me, Kennedy. In fact, I promise you that I'll make it as hard as I can."

My legs falter only for a moment as they carry me resolutely, albeit unsteadily, away from Reese.

CHAPTER SEVEN

REESE

There's no reason for me not to make plans for Kennedy's arrival on my yacht. Part of it is being sure of myself and my powers of persuasion. I've spent most of my life getting what I want. I've learned how to do it effectively, no matter who I'm negotiating with. But part of it is anticipation. I'm ready to get this show on the road. I'm anxious to spend some time getting to know this new Kennedy, the one who dances like she's dancing just for me. The one whose legs are longer than ever. The one whose lips are made just for mine. The one who I'm going to gorge myself on until I can't stand the sight of her.

I need to get Kennedy in my bed and out of my system as soon as possible.

Being the owner of the club at which she works, I have access to all of Kennedy's records—her mandatory health exams, including the results of her labs that show she's clean as a whistle; the brands of products she orders for her shows, from makeup to body glitter (which she never orders); her shoe and clothing sizes; and even the fact that she loves hats. I pass most of that information along to Kimmie, the woman in charge of the entertainment on my cruises. She can order outfits and accoutrements for Kennedy based on what she's worn in the past.

So, in essence, I have all the information I need to make sure Kennedy's room is prepared for her when she boards. And she *will* board. I was even able to get the son of a friend of my father's to find out if she has a passport that's up to date, which she does.

The last thing I have to do is let Kennedy know what time the car will be around to pick her up. I punch in the number that I got from her contact information sheet into my phone and listen to it ring.

"Hello?" comes a sleepy, husky voice.

"Mmmm, that sounds like an invitation," I murmur. And it does. It says to me that she's lying warm and naked beneath her sheets, her skin supple, her body willing.

After a short pause, during which I can almost hear Kennedy's eyes opening wider as she comes awake, she speaks. "Then you would be mistaken," she replies, prim and curt. She doesn't ask who's calling or mistake me for another man. She recognizes my voice, which means she's been thinking about me. Maybe remembering. Maybe wishing.

"Get someone to look after your cat for three months, and be packed and ready by four o'clock. I'll send someone to escort you to the airport. And bring your passport."

"How do you know I have a cat?"

"Educated guess."

She sniffs at my reply. "Aren't you being a little presumptuous?" she asks sharply.

"Not at all. You're a smart woman. You've looked at your options. You've weighed the merits of working the summer in my club and planning for the dream you may or may not achieve on your own, versus working for me and getting a once-in-a-lifetime audition that you could likely never get on your own, and you've concluded that there's only one sensible choice."

"Just like you knew I would," she says quietly.

I can't help but smile. I'm sure she hates that I've engineered the situation so perfectly. But if I didn't know how to make offers people can't refuse, I wouldn't be where I am today. I wouldn't be *who* I am today.

"Don't be too hard on yourself. There are very few people who can deny me."

"And, aside from me, who might those be?"

"You're not denying me."

"I'm taking you up on an offer, but you can rest assured that I'll be denying you in every other possible way."

"I guess we'll see, won't we?"

I hear her soft huff and I smile again. This might be even more fun than I anticipated. And I anticipated a whole hell of a lot!

Before she can argue further, I cut her off. "I'll see you at four."

I hang up.

I'm still smiling, thinking, planning when the phone rings in my hand. It's a number I don't recognize. The switch to Harrison Spencer is swift and automatic.

"Spencer," I answer brusquely.

"Mr. Spencer, my name is Oswold Bingham. I represent Malcolm Spencer's estate. Would you be available to attend the reading of his will today? You've been mentioned in a recently-notarized codicil."

I frown. I never expected to be named in Malcolm's will. It makes me feel even worse about my protracted absence.

"What time?"

"Three pm, sir. The reading will be done here at Bellano. In the study."

I don't bother to hide my sigh of irritation. "Fine, but I can only give you until 3:45. No later. I'm flying out this afternoon."

"I'll make sure to accommodate you then, sir. I'll be seeing you at three?"

"Yes," I respond.

"Thank you."

I hang up in a much pricklier mood than I was two minutes ago.

CHAPTER EIGHT

KENNEDY

As I shower and dress, I still question the wisdom of taking Reese up on his offer. It's a golden opportunity. All I have to do is just resist him long enough to make it off that boat and get what I came for.

Just resist him.

Like it's that easy.

Right.

Impulsively, I decide to visit Tanny. All my life, she's been my go-to person for advice. And comfort. And trustworthy friendship. Growing up at the back edge of Bellano with my foster father, Hank, in the grounds keeper's cottage left me with little in the way of playmates or companions that lived nearby, so Tanny was it.

And Reese.

For a while.

Out of habit, I drive around the property and park at my old house, one that now sits empty since Malcolm hired a company to care for the grounds. I walk the old, familiar trail through the woods, the one that bursts into the lush grass surrounding Bellano, right behind the garage at the kitchen door.

I rap my knuckles on the screen and wait for a response. Tanny is an early riser, but even if she weren't, eleven is plenty late for an impromptu visit.

Within a minute, I hear the click of a lock and the wooden door swings open, revealing Tanny's smiling face behind the screen between us.

"I was wondering when I'd see you," she says with a smile, flipping the latch on the screen so that I can enter.

"What made you think I'd come today?" I ask as I enter the kitchen. It smells just like it always has, like a mixture of something sweet baking, coffee and Malcolm's pipe tobacco. It's the most comforting aroma in the world.

"Yesterday was hard for all of us. In all kinds of different ways," she adds meaningfully, sending me a knowing look over her shoulder as she pours me a cup of coffee.

"Tanny, it was awful! He saw me dancing the other night. That was bad enough, but then to have to see him and talk to him...and for him to ask me to work on his boat..."

She turns around at that. "He asked you to work on his boat?"

"Yes. In exchange for getting me an audition with the Altman troupe. Can you believe that?"

Her smile is slight. "Yes, actually I can." I don't ask what she means by that. "Have you decided what you'll do?"

I sigh and circle my fingers over one throbbing temple. "I think so. I'm not sure it's the *right* thing, but I just can't see me letting an opportunity like this pass me by."

Tanny nods her head, sipping her coffee and holding her tongue.

"I mean, I got over Reese a long time ago. And this is work. Not to mention that it could mean a totally different future for me."

"That, it could," she agrees.

"Right?" I ask, looking for her validation and her encouragement, and maybe someone to tell me I'm doing the right thing.

"Will you be able to live with the regret of *not* taking this chance?"

"I learned a long time ago that I can live with a lot of regret and still survive, Tanny. But the thing is, do I need to? Can this really be as amazing as it seems? Or is it too good to be true?"

"What, exactly, are you worried about, Kennedy?" Tanny asks, setting her mug down and taking my free hand in both of hers.

"Oh, Tanny. I'm worried about *me*. I buried that poor girl who we all knew a long, long time ago, but..."

"But what? If you buried her, then there's nothing to worry about, is there?"

"I wouldn't think so if I just didn't feel so...so..."

"So what?"

"So drawn to him. God, it's like no amount of hate can kill what he does to me. What he's *always* done to me. But I know I can't trust him. He *is* a man, after all. Even if he makes me feel like no man ever has."

A look of sadness comes across Tanny's face. "Despite everything you've been through, despite all the reasons you have for feeling the way that you do, you can't go through life thinking you'll never find a man you can trust."

"It wouldn't be the end of the world." I try to keep my expression as unaffected as possible. But, like always, Tanny sees right through it.

She reaches over to squeeze my fingers. "But it's in all of us to want to find someone to share our lives with, to find someone to trust and love. Maybe you more than most."

"The girl in me used to think so, but now..."

"Maybe this will be good for you, Kennedy. Maybe you need to get some closure. For that girl you buried. *And* for the woman who took her place. You didn't become your strong self by hiding from adversity. You got this way by facing it. By overcoming. Don't let the past color your future. You're too smart to let that happen."

All my waffling seems silly now. "You're so right, Tanny." Impulsively, I lean over and hug her slight frame to mine. "He's just a man. *One man* who I used to know. He has no control over me unless I give it to him. I have nothing to fear. He's simply bringing me one step closer to my dream. That's all."

"One step closer to your dream," Tanny repeats, patting my cheek reassuringly. The funny thing is, I get the feeling that she's speaking about much more than just my dancing.

CHAPTER NINE

REESE

I head to Bellano a few minutes before the reading of the will. As I'm pulling into my old spot beside the garage, I see the flash of a familiar chestnut head ducking into the woods to my right.

Kennedy. She's been on my mind so much for the last thirty-six hours; I'd recognize that head anywhere now.

I'm curious as to why she was here, but I'm also ten times more distracted than I was to begin with. Knowing she's in the forest right now...so near the place where I took her virginity all those years ago...all alone in the privacy of the trees... God, it makes me throb—the desire to taste how time has matured and sweetened that delectable body of hers.

Damn.

With a muffled growl, I get out of the car and head around to the kitchen entrance. I glance up at the window as I approach the steps. Force of habit. But this time Tanny *is* standing there, like she used to be, smiling at me as I ascend the stairs.

If I had to guess, I'd say she's still in the kitchen after having talked to Kennedy.

"Good morning, handsome boy." Tanny greets me with a smile, a kiss to the cheek and a cup of coffee as I walk through the door.

"Good morning," I reply, returning her gesture. The smell of garden flowers drifts up to tickle my nose and remind me of all the happy childhood memories I have with Tanny. When I lean back to look down at her, her blue eyes are shining brightly. Happily. She looks more like herself—younger, attractive, loving. Maybe the worst of Malcolm's death has passed. "You're looking well."

She smiles, glancing down at her crisp white blouse and navy blue slacks, and brushing away an imaginary piece of lint. "Why, thank you. I've been called in for the reading of the will as well, and I...I..."

I curl my fingers around her thin upper arms. "It'll be fine, Tanny. I promise." Her smile is only a little sad today.

"I know it will, my sweet. One way or the other."

I take a sip of my coffee. "So, have you had company this morning?"

"As a matter of fact I have," she confirms. "And now I get some more. My two favorite people, two days in a row. I couldn't be happier."

"Yes, I thought I saw Kennedy leaving. What did she want?"

Tanny laughs. "She was just visiting. Is that allowed, Mr. Nosey?"

I smile, wanting to press her for information, but knowing I'd better not. Tanny is the type of person that needs a soft approach. To be such a sweet and loving woman, she can be quite stubborn when she decides she doesn't want to do something. Despite her appearance, she's a tough woman, so I can't come at her straight on. "I'm sorry. Of course it is. I haven't kept up with Kennedy much in the last several years, so I was just curious. That's all."

"She's been doing just fine. Couldn't be prouder of the young woman she's become. She went through pure hell, but she didn't let it break her. She's made of stronger stuff than what it looks like."

"Pure hell? What's that all about?" That piques my curiosity even more.

Tanny begins to shake her head. "Those aren't my stories to tell. If you really want to know, you'll have to ask her yourself. Even then, I'm not sure she'd want you to know. That's for her to decide."

Now I *really* want to press her, but I know it won't do me any good. Tanny has a fierce sense of loyalty. Normally, that extends to me, but it also extends to Kennedy. I know this from years gone by. So, between the two of us, she'll betray neither one.

Damn.

"Well, I'm sure I'll find a chance. She'll be working for me on one of my cruises."

"She will, will she?" Tanny asks with a sly grin.

I falter for a split second. "Yes. Or did she tell you something different?"

Tanny's grin melts into a kind smile. "No, she didn't tell me any different. I just don't think you should make too many assumptions or take too many things for granted with her. She's not the same girl you knew all those years ago, Harrison."

"She's an adult, Tanny. I'm sure she is perfectly capable of making decisions for herself. And dealing with the consequences."

"Maybe *she's* not the one I'm worried about."

****

I glance at my watch again. Along with Tanny, myself and my father, there are various other attorneys and representatives present. We are all waiting, albeit impatiently, for Malcolm's lawyer to arrive. He's nearly twenty minutes late already. At this rate, I'll be leaving before he even gets here.

Across the table, I see my father glance at his watch within seconds of me glancing at mine. I resist the urge to curl my lip at our likeness. I don't *want* to be anything like him. But I am. I know I am. To some degree, it was inevitable. I learned from him. From watching him, listening to him, being around him. It's times like this when I see the similarities and I abhor every single one of them. I just haven't yet found a good enough reason to change things. After all, Henslow Spencer is very successful. And, at this point, that's my biggest motivator—*having* more, *achieving* more, *being* more. Just...more.

With a muffled thump, the door behind me opens. I don't turn to see who entered. I just know it had better be the lawyer or I'm outta here.

A robust man wearing a wool jacket with leather on the elbows makes his way to the only empty chair at the round mahogany table. He sets his briefcase atop it, making eye contact with each of us and nodding a silent greeting. After he's retrieved a thick manila folder from inside his case, he snaps shut the locks and sets it on the floor, clearing his throat before he begins.

"Sorry for the delay, gentlemen. There were some...last-minute details that needed my attention, but now I'm ready to execute this, the last will and testament of Malcolm Henry Spencer."

No one speaks as he opens the folder and rifles through papers, pulling out one document with a light blue backing.

As he begins formally reading the will, I suppress the urge to sigh in bored frustration. It's not that I'm not grateful for whatever my uncle Malcolm left me. I was closer to him than practically anybody for the first half of my life. It's just that I have other things—and other people—on my mind, making it hard for me to sit patiently through something like this when I'd much rather be sitting across from Kennedy. Watching her. Studying her. Formulating a plan for getting her back in my bed with the greatest speed.

Mr. Bingham gets my full attention with the mention of my name.

"In deference to Mr. Harrison Spencer's departure schedule, I'll begin with the family estate known to all as Bellano. Per Malcolm's wishes, 'The estate will be left, in equal parts ownership, to my nephew, Harrison Ronaldo Spencer, or his closest living relative, and Mary Elizabeth Spencer or her closest living relative. All decisions regarding the grounds, the estate holdings and the upkeep will be made jointly, with the exception of the presence of Mrs. Judith E. Tannenbaum, whom I hereby grant a life estate at Bellano'."

When Bingham pauses to continue, hushed whispers break out around the table. I'm as surprised as everyone else to hear that Malcolm left Bellano to me, but, also like everyone else, I'm *very* surprised to hear of a female Spencer relative being named as well. Since its existence, Bellano has never been left to a woman, much less one who no one has ever heard of.

It's my father who finally asks the question on everyone's mind. "Who, exactly, is Mary Elizabeth Spencer?"

Mr. Bingham glances nervously around the table. "Malcolm had this codicil drawn up just weeks prior to his death. I was out of town, so my partner did the work for him. Unfortunately, being unfamiliar with the family, he didn't get any more information on Ms. Spencer, so I'm still in the process of locating her."

"Well, you'd better make quick work of it, Bingham, because if you can't produce this supposed heir, a woman with whom none of us are familiar, you can bet your ass I'll be contesting this will. Bellano is the

Spencer family home, and it will stay with the *real* Spencers if I have to take it to the Supreme Court to see that it does."

I catch movement from the corner of my eye and glance over to see Tanny drop her head and close her eyes. I'm sure she's thinking it's a shame that grown men have to act like this only days after the death of a loved one. And over possessions, no less. It makes me feel ashamed for being so much like my father.

"Mr. Spencer, I assure you—"

"I don't trust that you can assure me of anything, *Mr. Bingham,*" my father snaps.

I look at Tanny's pale face again and it spurs me into action.

"Mr. Bingham, will that be all the need you have of me or Mrs. Tannenbaum? If so, I think we'd both like to get on with our plans for the day." The least I can do is spare Tanny any more of this unpleasantness. "Please forward copies of the will to my attorney. You have his information already, I believe."

When I glance back at Tanny, she's watching me with watery, grateful eyes. I smile at her and she gives me a subtle, regal nod of acknowledgment.

"Yes, I do. And yes, this is the only part that pertains to either of you. It's my understanding that Malcolm has already given to Mrs. Tannenbaum any of his possessions that he wanted her to have. Is that accurate, Mrs. Tannenbaum?"

"Yes, it is," comes her quiet reply.

No one in the room argues. Whatever Malcolm saw fit to give Tanny is still probably less than she deserves for staying with him all these years. Even my cold, hard father knows that.

"In that case, I think we'll be on our way." I stand and walk to Tanny's chair, pulling it back as she comes to her feet. "Gentleman." I give the room a glancing nod and then I escort Tanny out the door.

Once we've left the study and all the tension there behind us, I turn to Tanny. "Do you know who this Mary Elizabeth is? Did Malcolm ever mention her?"

Tanny raises her face to mine and I notice how ashen she is. "Harrison, would you mind if I went to lie down? I believe I might have a migraine coming on. Just the stress of the last few days…"

She lays a shaking hand on my arm and starts to walk off, even before I can reply. Bending, I sweep her into my arms. "I'll carry you," I tell her simply, walking the short distance down the hall to her room at the back of the house, nearest Malcolm's.

It looks just like it did when I was last here all those years ago. Antique furnishings covered in faded rose-and-cream colored fabrics, a fresh flower arrangement sitting on the dresser and a book lying on the night table right beside her reading glasses. Everything in this room is elegant, womanly and one hundred percent Tanny.

Gently, I deposit her on the bed and then move to the windows behind it, drawing the blinds shut. Before I leave, I bend to kiss Tanny's cool cheek.

"Rest. You have my number if you need anything. I'll come and stay for a few weeks when I get back into the country. But if something happens and you need me before then, call. Okay?"

She nods.

"Promise me."

Her smile is small. "I promise."

"I'll get all this straightened out. Don't worry over it."

Her smile deepens. "I won't worry. You go on. Have a good time with Kennedy."

"So she *is* coming?" I feel relieved. Tanny was a bit vague earlier.

"Yes, I believe she's coming."

"I'll take good care of her, Tanny."

She reaches up to pinch my chin. "You'd better, young man."

I laugh. "God forbid I suffer the wrath of Tanny."

"Just so long as you know," she says with a grin before she waves me out the door. "Now, you go on. Have a safe trip. And have fun."

I don't tell her how much fun I plan to have. I only smile as I pull the door shut behind me.

CHAPTER TEN

KENNEDY

I shouldn't have waited until the last minute to pack. I guess I was hoping for a sign that I'm doing the right thing. But I didn't get one, so I've been left to muddle through the decision-making process the best that I can. In the end, I go with my gut. All my other gauges lie in direct contradiction to one another. My head says I'm strong and I can do this. My heart says I'm crazy to risk being around Reese again. Those two still haven't reached an agreement, so that's why I had to consult another faculty—my gut. And it says that I can do this, that I need to go for the dream. This could be my only chance to chase it with any hope of catching it.

But my gut can't tell me what to pack. I mean, Reese has told me virtually nothing about this cruise. I throw a variety of clothes into my suitcase, along with my toiletries and a couple of swimsuits just in case. I stand staring at it for at least five minutes as I rack my brain for other things I might need. Giving up when I can think of nothing but the way it felt to have Reese touch my face again, I decide it might be prudent to just *ask*. But rather than calling, I take the coward's way out and I text Reese instead.

Me: What do I need to pack? I don't know where we're going or what I'll need, work-wise.

As I'm waiting for his response, Bozey, my calico-colored Maine Coon cat, weaves a warm figure eight around my legs as if to remind me not to forget about making arrangements for him. I reach down to scoop him up and he drapes bonelessly over my arm.

"I could never forget about you, Bozey." I nuzzle his nose with mine. He twitches his ears, letting me know that I'm pushing the personal space boundaries, but otherwise he tolerates it pretty well. He's a very good cat and I already feel guilty about leaving him. "Clive will take good care of you," I tell him, referring to my elderly neighbor who loves Bozey almost as much as I do. Bozey loves him, too.

I give Bozey an extra nuzzle for good measure just as the bleep of my phone alerts me to an incoming text. It's Reese. His response is not terribly surprising.

For a man.

A *ladies'* man.

Reese: As far as I'm concerned you don't have to pack any clothes. Consider clothing optional any time you're in my company.

I can easily picture his gorgeous grin and the devilish light in his aqua eyes, and some small part of me melts a little. Just a little.

I steel myself against it, against *him*. As I will continue to do for the next several weeks until I can put Reese behind me. Again. Maybe for good this time.

Me: Warm weather? Cold weather? Do I need to bring clothes to dance in? And will you have uniforms for the service staff?

I'm trying to keep it professional, whether that's the way he wants it or not. Tough shit.

Reese: Warm weather. Bring what you want to wear. Your work clothing is taken care of.

In my head, my response is brusque, yet professional.

Me: That's what I wanted to know. Thank you.

Even when his is not.

Reese: Of course. I'm happy to answer all your questions and take care of ALL your needs.

I debate for a moment whether I should respond, but then I do, unable to resist another opportunity to set him straight on where this is and is *not* going.

Me: You won't be getting anywhere near my needs.

When I read his reply, I can almost *hear* the sexy dripping from his tone.

Reese: Then I suppose I'll just have to bring your needs to me.

Ignoring the little chill that spreads down my arms, I decide the prudent thing, at this point, would be to quit while I'm ahead. *Telling* Reese is obviously not enough. I'll have to trust that *showing* him will be.

CHAPTER ELEVEN

REESE

As I walk to the door of unit seven in the small, brick townhouse complex, I notice the curtain flutter in the window of the adjacent unit. When I glance to my right, I see an older man's face staring back at me from one corner of the glass. I nod politely. He nods in return. He watches me until I reach the stoop in front of Kennedy's door, a step that effectively removes me from his line of sight.

Another man bewitched by Kennedy, I think with a wry smile. She's probably got more than her fair share of admirers. And I can't blame a single one of them.

I knock on the door and step back to lean against one of the thick white columns that holds up her porch. I hear some bumping and thumping before the door flies open to reveal an out-of-breath Kennedy.

"I thought you were sending a car or something?" she pants, blowing a few strands of silky hair out of one eye.

I turn to look back at my sleek black car parked in one of the two spots directly in front of her unit. "Last time I checked, that's what I arrived in."

"But I thought...I mean, it sounded like... Oh, never mind," she stammers, waving a hand dismissively as she reaches just inside the door for an enormous suitcase. With a grunt, she hefts it over the threshold and lets it drop like a cement block onto the stoop. "I'm almost ready. Hang on."

With that, she disappears inside again. The door is still open, so I can see her as she darts around her living room, straightening the pillows on the olive green couch and picking up a speck of something from the red rug beneath it. She stops and looks around, likely going over some kind of mental checklist. When she's satisfied, she tosses whatever was in her hand into the trash can, bends to scratch her cat behind his ears and tells him he's a good boy, and that she'll miss him.

I can't help but notice the way her jeans show off her long, slender legs and cup her round ass to perfection. I know what that ass looks like. The glimpse I got of it the night she danced is permanently etched onto my brain.

I feel a groan build somewhere deep in my gut.

When she comes toward the door, I don't move. I stay leaning against the column as she locks the knob and the deadbolt, jiggles the handle and then backs up to wave at her neighbor, the guy I saw peeking through the curtains.

Finally she turns back to face me. "Ready?"

Her cheeks are flushed, her eyes are bright and there's a breathless quality to her voice that's making it very hard for me to keep my hands off her.

"Oh, I'm very ready," I tell her as I straighten, reaching out to remove a strand of hair that has strayed into her lip gloss. "The question is: Are you?"

She watches me intently. She knows exactly what I'm asking. I can tell by the way she finally tips up her chin and meets my eyes so boldly. She surprises me by laughing. "Trust me, you don't need to be worrying about *me*."

Her bravado is belied only by the dilation of her pupils and the slight tremor to her lips. She wants to think she has it all under control, that resisting me will be a piece of cake. But, deep down, she knows there's something between us. And that it's inevitable.

Making her admit it is going to be the fun part.

CHAPTER TWELVE

KENNEDY

I watch Reese discreetly from the corner of my eye as he guides his powerful, expensive car back to the highway. So many things are exactly as I remember them. The shade of his eyes. The unruly wave to his hair when it gets too long. The shape of his lips and the way he purses them when he's concentrating.

But, on the other hand, so many things have changed. He's older, harder, more worldly. He's a stranger to me now. But still, there's something about him... Even *I* can feel it. Something that tugs at me constantly.

Reese is still the handsomest man I've ever seen. Dark, slightly wavy hair, piercing aqua eyes, long lashes. His skin is smooth and tan, his nose straight, his cheekbones high. His mouth is a perfectly-sculpted bow in the center of his square jaw. God, he's beautiful. Wealthy. Powerful. Charming. He was irresistible as a young adult, but now...women don't stand a chance. The only reason I do is because we have history. Bad history. My scars keep my focus where it needs to be.

Mostly.

His big hands rest on the steering wheel with confident ease. I look away from them because they remind me of things I'd rather not think about. Things that make my stomach feel tight and achy.

When he reaches cruising speed on the highway, he glances over at me, grinning slightly when he finds me watching him.

"Penny for your thoughts," he says softly.

"I was just thinking how much you've changed."

"In fourteen years?" he laughs. "Yeah, I've changed. But so have you."

To this, I just nod, turning to look out my window.

When I don't move to continue the conversation, Reese does. "How have you been, Kennedy? Fill me in on your life for the last decade and a half."

There is so much to say, yet nothing at all. He missed it. Every bit of it. When he left. Therefore he has no right to it. Not even to my memories of it.

"Not much to tell. I became a dancer. At one of your clubs."

He is unflappable. "How did you know you wanted to dance?"

"I've always wanted to dance."

"You never told me."

"There were a lot of things I never told you, Reese."

"So tell me now."

"Why? What's the point?" I turn to look at him. My voice is angry, which frustrates me. I don't want him to know he got a rise out of me. "I mean, we don't need to do this. I'll be working for you. Everything you need to know about me is in an employee file somewhere."

"Nothing that I want to know about you is in an employee file."

"Then maybe you need to keep better records."

Much to my dismay, Reese laughs, sending a little shiver of recognition down my spine. That sound…I always loved that rich, deep sound.

"That's great advice. I think I'll start now. So, how did you end up at my club?"

I sigh. Obviously this is not something he's going to let go of easily. "I met a girl who dances there. She told me what it was like, that no one takes their clothes off. At least not many of them, and that we can be creative with our routines as long as they're sexy. I liked the idea of being able to dance the way I want to, to wear what I feel comfortable in. So, she put in a good word with the manager, he let me audition and hired me on the spot. End of story."

"I knew I liked that guy," Reese mumbles, sending me a wink that curls my toes. Silently, I curse each tiny digit for not being stronger. "What are you thinking when you do that?"

"Do what?"

"Pucker your lips and frown like that. I noticed you doing it yesterday at Malcolm's."

His question takes me by surprise, giving way to me answering more honestly than I should. "I don't know about yesterday, but I was just cursing my toes."

"For what?"

I don't answer, but I feel my cheeks sting in embarrassment.

You walked right into that one, dumb ass!

"So is this how it's going to be for three months?"

I turn to give him my full attention and my most serious expression. "Yes. It is."

"You know it doesn't have to be."

"Oh, yes it does."

"Why?"

"I told you I'm not interested in anything but you getting me an audition with Altman. I'll hold up my end of the bargain, but that doesn't include answering your questions."

"Why are you being like this?"

This irritates me, so I slap my hands down on my thighs. "Because we had our shot, Reese, and it didn't work out. End of story. This...this...arrangement is only temporary. It's serving a purpose for both of us. Nothing more."

He doesn't say anything for a few minutes. His face is set in a pensive expression. He's not angry or offended, just thoughtful.

"I'll change your mind, Kennedy. One way or the other."

My stomach twists into a knot. I can only imagine how persuasive Reese can be. But still, I don't give in. I can't. "You might as well save your energy. It won't work."

After a long pause, he speaks again. "You were right," he says enigmatically.

"About what?"

Reese gives me his brightest smile. "I have changed."

When he doesn't continue, I ask, "What's that supposed to mean?"

There's still a sexy, devastating curve to his lips. "You'll see."

I let the silence stretch between us, mainly because arguing with Reese is turning out to be a lesson in futility.

CHAPTER THIRTEEN

REESE

I drive onto the tarmac of the private airstrip that I use for the jet I timeshare. A guy from the service is waiting beside the extended steps of the craft. I know that he's from the service I use because he's dressed entirely in white. From his button-up shirt and blazer to his sharply-creased slacks and spotless shoes, everything is white.

When I pull to a stop near him, he moves to open the door for Kennedy. After she's on her feet, he scrambles around to my side. I step out and hand him my keys along with a folded bill. He takes them with a silent nod and I reach for Kennedy. I put my hand on the small of her back and lead her to the retractable stairs. I feel her flinch at my touch, but she doesn't move away. I suppress a smile. I know she still reacts to me. I don't have to feel it beneath my fingertips to know it. But damn, how I want to.

As the attendant loads our bags from the trunk into the luggage compartment of the jet, Kennedy and I make our way into the main cabin area. Hemi, Sloane and Sig are already on board. I'm not surprised when Kennedy takes one of the empty chairs rather than sitting on the other empty couch. It's the only way she can ensure that I don't sit beside her. Close enough to touch. And that's fine with me. The time is coming when she won't be able to so easily avoid me. And, although I'm not a patient man, for this, I can wait. For *her*, I can wait. In fact, that might make the end result even sweeter.

CHAPTER FOURTEEN

KENNEDY

I get situated in the plush, ivory-leather chair, setting my purse at my feet and crossing my legs before I glance around at my flight companions. From the corner of my eye, I see Reese sink into the thick cushions of a loveseat and throw one arm along the back. I make a point not to look directly at him. I'm discovering the less I can do that, the better off I am.

"Kennedy, this is Hemi, my brother, and his girlfriend, Sloane. The gentleman to the left is her brother, Sig." I give each person he mentions a smile and I get one from each of them in return.

I finally get to meet Hemi. Although Reese talked about him some when we were kids, Hemi didn't visit his uncle much and I never got to meet him. I would've remembered that because He. Is. Gorgeous.

Just like his brother. There is no denying that they are related. They both have the same dark hair, the same skin tone, the same stunning smile, only Hemi's eyes appear to be a different, darker shade of blue, like navy almost. One dark brow is pierced and I can see a tattoo of some sort peeking out from beneath the bottom edge of his t-shirt sleeve. He has bad boy written all over him, and it's no wonder Sloane fell for him, especially when he turns his eyes back to her. They fairly glow with his adoration, something else I can easily see. Sloane is beautiful in a young, fresh way. And she obviously worships the ground Hemi walks on. I can't help the little ribbon of jealousy that works its way through me. They have what every girl dreams of.

Until she gets her heart broken and realizes that, in the absence of that kind of true and perfect love, there is only devastation, on one end or the other. Having experienced that once is enough to deter me from ever looking for it again.

I turn my eyes and my smile to Sig. He's extremely handsome as well, with his dark hair and chocolate eyes so much like his sister's. Only he's all man, hard where she is soft. Even sitting, I can see that he's enormous. I'd guess when he stands that he's at least six feet five inches of hard muscle and cute, sexy grin.

All in all, I feel old and ugly by comparison, which does nothing for my confidence or my mood. I can feel myself withdrawing almost immediately.

"Kennedy and I grew up together," Reese tells the group.

"We won't hold that against you, Kennedy," Sig says with a flirtatious wink. He swivels his chair to face me more fully and raises one dark brow as his eyes flicker over me. "And will you be joining us on the boat?"

"I will. I'll be working, though."

"Doing what?"

"I guess I'll be your...entertainment," I explain, trying not to let that make me feel like the hired trash. Consciously, I lift my chin and keep my smile in place, reminding myself that I have nothing to be ashamed of. I dance for a living. At least I'm working toward my dream. Some of us just have to take the long, hard road. That's all.

"Oh, really?" Sig asks, interest evident in his tone. "And just how will you be entertaining us?" The look of appreciation in his eye makes me feel less self-conscious, and his friendly, harmlessly flirtatious nature puts me right at ease. I like him instantly.

"I'm a dancer."

Sig leans up, very openly interested now. "God, that Reese is a lucky bastard."

"And why is that?"

"He gets all the hot women around here."

"Oh, it's not like that. We...uh...we're just old friends. And I actually work for him in one of his clubs."

"Which one?"

"*Exotique.*"

Sig's mouth drops open a little bit. "Holy shit! You're that hottie from the other night, aren't you?

With the shirt and the hat? Dayum, you were amazing!"

I can't help but blush at his enthusiastic and appreciative response. "Thank you. But I won't *only* be dancing. I'll be doing some serving as well, from what I understand."

I look to Reese for confirmation and am taken aback by the look of anger and irritation on his face.

"I haven't decided exactly what you'll be doing yet," he says tightly.

After a short, tense silence, Sig speaks again and I look back at him, ignoring Reese and his fuming. "Well, if you have down time, maybe you could teach me a few moves. You know, some private instruction."

The grin that Sig gives me makes his pick-up line more adorably charming than offensive, so I laugh. "I don't give *those* kinds of dances."

"Well, that's a damn shame. But if you ever change your mind, I'd be happy to lend you my lap or help you with your costumes. You know, whatever you need. I'm a public servant at heart."

His wide, voracious smile draws another laugh from me. "I get the impression that you're quite incorrigible."

"If that's code for strong, protective, and handsome as hell, then you couldn't be more right."

And so it goes with Sig. He has an answer for everything and a totally charming way of turning all my comments into sexual innuendos, which is both flattering and entertaining.

He stimulates my laugh more than anyone or anything has in years. Enjoying his company and his audacious flirting is easy as pie, especially considering how virtually *any* interaction with Reese keeps me torn up in one way or another. It's no hardship on my part to let Sig dominate my time and attention during the flight to the west coast.

But every time I sneak a glance at Reese, which happens more often than I'd like or than I intend, I can't stop the equal parts of pleasure and pain that course through me. At times, it's like nothing has changed.

But everything has.

CHAPTER FIFTEEN

REESE

When another flight attendant makes her way to me, I find it hard to keep my short temper in check.

"Would you like something else to drink, Mr. Spencer?" she asks quietly.

"Not right now," is my clipped reply.

She leans forward ever so slightly and drops her voice a little lower. "Is there anything else I could get you or do for you?"

I take my eyes off Kennedy's profile long enough to give the attendant my full attention. This one has flown with me before. The jet is part of a timeshare between me, my father and two other business associates with frequent travel needs. The company that we use for flight crew knows that I have specific requirements of the female attendants. My clientele like all their staffing encounters to be visually pleasurable and the company we use has always been accommodating. They are screened thoroughly and regularly, just like all my club employees are, and these women are young, beautiful and, occasionally, very willing to go...above and beyond. Like this one.

I see the heat in her dark blue eyes. I see the way she wets her lips and squeezes her breasts together for maximum cleavage. She's just as appealing as any girl I'd hire if I had my pick. But not today. Today she's just annoying. Today she's not what I want. Today she's just not Kennedy.

"As...enjoyable as that sounds, I think I'm set for the flight," I tell her kindly.

She nods and straightens before moving back through the cabin to ask the others if they'd like something to eat or drink. My eyes shift to Kennedy again and I see that she's watching me. She's not smiling at something Sig said or talking to him like she's known *him* forever. No, this time *I've* got her full attention. And she's not laughing.

I give her a small nod before I turn my attention to the view outside the window. I don't even bother to hide the smile that I suddenly feel like wearing.

Damn her, two can play that game.

I let my irritation dissolve into calm determination. If there's one thing that life has taught me, it's to never give up. If things aren't going my way, I do something to shift the tide. If the first answer is no, I keep trying until I get the right one. And if something gets in my way, I've learned to move it *out* of my way. Kennedy may not admit that she'll be mine again yet, but she will. I'll see to it.

My cruise assistant, Karesh, is waiting for us with the limo at the airport. He is capable, reliable and a stickler for the details, which is a combination that I consider mandatory for someone in his position. He knows how I like things and he makes sure they are prepared in such a way, down to the letter.

We quietly discuss all the arrangements as everyone else chats on the way to Marina del Rey. He's already arranged for the smaller boat that will ferry us from there to where the yacht is moored out in the deeper waters.

When the driver pulls up beside the dock, I can see that the ferrying boat is already taking our luggage out to the yacht.

Hemi comes to stand beside me, slapping me on the back as he points out toward the yacht where it floats out in the bay. "Is that the new yacht, bro?"

"No, the new one is registered in the Caribbean. This is the second one I bought."

Sloane steps up to stand beside Hemi, winding her arms around his waist. After a few seconds she looks out in the direction of the yacht, too. "Ohmigod, is that it? Is that the boat we'll be going to Hawaii on?" Her voice is dripping with excitement.

"Yep, that's it," he tells her. She turns shining eyes up at him and he gives her a quick kiss.

"This is gonna be awesome, baby!" she beams.

He nods and kisses her forehead, the moment turning suddenly intimate. I clear my throat and take a few steps away. With perfect timing, the ferrying boat returns from the yacht to retrieve us. I give my hands one loud slap. "Let's load up so we can get going," I tell them, anxious to be on our way.

Karesh ushers Hemi, Sloane and Sig down the dock to where the smaller boat waits. I look back for Kennedy who is trailing behind. She's walking slowly, staring out at the horizon with a frown on her face.

"Is something wrong?" I ask.

She says nothing at first, simply continues to stare. Finally, she turns cloudy eyes to me. "That is *your* boat? The one I'll be spending the summer on?"

"It is."

"So this is what your life is like? I had no idea."

"This is just one of my businesses. This isn't where I live my life. It's simply what I do."

Kennedy's eyes stare into mine. "In your case, I think it's pretty much the same thing, don't you?"

She seems unhappy as she walks away. I don't quite know what to make of her commentary, so I let it go. No sense in wasting time on things I can't figure out or control. Especially not when I need to put my energy toward the things that I *can*.

CHAPTER SIXTEEN

KENNEDY

A pleasant yet quiet man named Karesh gives us a tour of the yacht.

"This is Domani, the second of Mr. Spencer's three entertainment yachts."

"What does that mean, 'Domani'?" Sloane asks, reading my mind.

"It means, 'tomorrow'," Karesh explains. "His first is called 'Ieri' which means yesterday, and his newest is called 'Sempre'," he finishes.

"Forever," I whisper. I remember hearing the Italian word somewhere, maybe from Malcolm. I think I remember him saying his mother was born in Sicily, which would account for the dark good looks of all the Spencer men.

We follow Karesh from one stunning space on the yacht to another, all set against the backdrop of an endless horizon and water as far as the eye can see. We've already left the harbor and I had no idea we were even moving.

It's more opulent than anything I've ever seen. The accommodations include everything from a library and show room, to a small swimming pool and gym. Although more compact, this craft lacks nothing that any resort on land boasts. At least not that I can see.

I wonder how I ever, in my young mind, thought that Reese and I could have a future of any kind. We might as well be from different planets. I mean, I knew it at the time. I knew he was the quintessential rich kid and I was the classic poor girl, but this…this is just staggering. We weren't worlds apart; we were galaxies apart. I was a fool to ever get involved with someone like Reese. But the only thing I can do about it now is vow never to make the same mistake again.

And I don't plan to.

Ever.

When we go below decks to the staterooms, Karesh begins assigning rooms. I get a glimpse inside each one we pass. They're all outfitted with queen sized beds, rich cream duvets and carpeting that appears to be six inches thick. They're nicer than my bedroom at home, which I was quite proud of until today.

Soon, everyone is getting settled in their room and I am following Karesh by myself to another part of the ship.

"These are the crew quarters," he says. "And since you'll be *working* for Mr. Spencer during this voyage, your accommodations will be located here." We pass several narrow doors, one of which is open and I can see inside. Two sets of bunk beds dominate the room, one against the wall to the left, the other against the wall to the right. I gulp. I'm a very private person and it really didn't occur to me to ask about living quarters. But, it's too late to ask now. We've already left Los Angeles behind.

We pass an area he explains is the crew lounge. It's a large room with a kitchenette against the back wall and a long table that separates it from the living area. The main space holds three sofas, two chairs, and a big screen television that's mounted to the wall. Several people are gathered around two men playing at a foosball table that's pushed into a corner. None of them bother to look up as we pass, for which I'm intensely grateful. I need to get my bearings before meeting the others.

Karesh continues on to more rooms, finally stopping beside the very last door. He opens it and sweeps his arm forward, an indication that I should precede him. So I do.

This room is different than the others. It's lighter, this one having a small, high window on one wall, and it has one full-sized bed rather than the bunk beds that line the walls in the others. There is a small sink in one corner, as well as a soft round chair that appears to be bolted to the floor. I hold my breath, almost afraid to ask if this one will be mine.

"This is where you'll be staying," Karesh divulges.

"Really?" He nods his head and smiles.

"Really."

I chew on the inside of my cheek, running my hand over the countertop that surrounds the sink. "Please don't take this as a complaint, but why do I get a room like this? What about the other rooms?"

"Mr. Spencer asked that you be given this room."

"Did he say why?"

"I only do as I'm told, ma'am. I don't ask questions."

I nod and smile. "I understand. Well, thank you. This room is...is...it's great."

"I'm glad you approve," he says pleasantly. "Your bags will be here shortly. If there is anything else you need, feel free to ask. Just dial 300 from any phone on the ship. I can arrange to have any necessities obtained for you once we reach Hawaii."

"We're going to Hawaii?"

"Yes, that's our first stop, where we'll drop off Mr. Spencer's brother and his companions and pick up our clients."

"Oh, I see. And then where will we be going?"

"French Polynesia, ma'am," he answers.

"Oh," I reply vaguely but enthusiastically. I have no idea what kinds of destinations lie in French Polynesia. That's what happens when you don't finish high school. The GED program skips a lot. "It sounds amazing."

"Oh, it is," he assures. "I'll leave you to freshen up. If your bags aren't delivered in ten minutes—"

He doesn't even have time to finish his sentence before he's interrupted by a young, fit, blond guy. "Sir, I have them."

"Perfect timing, Brian," Karesh says, stepping out of his way. "Brian, this is Kennedy. She'll be in entertainment. Serving as well if extra help is needed. Kennedy, this is Brian. He's the on-board trainer and the person who will be keeping you conditioned during your stay."

"It's nice to meet you, Brian."

"Likewise," Brian says with a broad smile.

Karesh nods to me. "I'll see you in one hour for dinner in the rotunda."

"Thank you, Karesh," I say before he walks off. Smiling, I turn to Brian who's holding my big suitcase. "I'll take that."

As if it weighs nothing, Brian picks up the case with one hand, keeping it out of my reach as he holds me off with the other. "Nope. I've got it. I'll be working those muscles of yours soon enough."

He gives me an engaging smile as he walks past me to deposit my suitcase on the bed. He turns, dusting off his hands, and winks at me. "Welcome aboard, Dorothy. You're not in Kansas anymore."

I'm surprised when he kisses my cheek on his way back out the door. I'm sure I'm wearing an expression that says as much as he closes the door behind himself, leaving me standing in the middle of my new room, pondering his strangely familiar behavior.

In the quiet moments following his departure, I realize three things about Brian. One, I don't think he meant anything derogatory by the Dorothy comment. Two, something in my gut tells me he's gay. And three, I like him already. That seemingly-innocuous trio of tiny details puts me at ease and gives me a better outlook on the coming summer than any I've had so far.

Finding someone that I can be friends with has never been easy for me. Trust issues aside, I'm reserved right up to the moment I feel very comfortable in someone's presence, which makes it difficult for people to get to know and like me. It's something I learned long ago and have come to terms with. It's also something that has made me appreciate those who I *can* call "friend," those who gave me a chance, who stuck it out until I loosened up. They've turned out to be some of the best people I've had the good fortune of filling my life with, and I treasure them. It's probably no coincidence that they're all older people, like Tanny, Malcolm and Clive. I get the feeling that I'll soon be adding the much-younger Brian to that list, though. And I'd like nothing more than to be right. We'll see how that goes. But for now, he's managed to make me feel welcome and at ease, and I desperately needed that.

I go about getting settled in my room, quickly discovering that there are all sorts of interesting uses of space, like storage for instance. There are drawers tucked under the bed and under the sink, which is a good thing. I didn't bring *that much* stuff, but I wouldn't have enough room to store it all if I'd been given one of the group rooms, especially once I see that the closet is full of clothes already.

I can only assume they are for me. Not only are they brand new and all in my size, but they look like things I'd wear to dance. My style exactly. Whoever Reese has working for him is very good!

Among the costumes, though, are some beautiful gowns and very nice formal wear. I don't know what I'm expected to wear the items for, but I suppose someone will tell me when the time comes. For all I know, Reese may have his service staff wear things like that. On a boat like this, nothing would surprise me.

But for tonight, my first night on board with no idea what to expect at dinner, I dress in something of my own—a pair of soft moleskin pants in chocolate and a sleeveless blouse in cream. It's the kind of outfit that can be worn in a wide variety of situations without making me stand out.

I brush out my hair until it hangs in shiny waves around my shoulders and give my lips a fresh coat of gloss. Other than that, I'm going as is. I have no one to impress.

After only five minutes of being cooped up in my tiny room with a window that I can't see out of unless I stand on the bed, I'm already too fidgety to stay here until dinner time. I decide to go up to one of the open-air decks to enjoy the view instead.

I make three wrong turns getting from where my room is in the forward-most part of the ship to where I thought the steps were that lead to the upper decks. Luckily, one of my wrong turns leads me to a set of steps that end up in the kitchen where Brian just happens to be standing, talking to a man whom I assume is the chef. His tall, puffy hat and long white apron are dead giveaways.

Brian smiles as soon as I appear in the doorway just beyond the long, stainless steel table at which they stand. He's going over a list of foods as the chef winds long, thin strips of dough into spirals.

"Well, look at you," he says pleasantly, bestowing upon me another of his winning, yet markedly un-sexually-interested smiles.

"I think I'm lost. I was actually going up to one of the decks to take in some fresh air before dinner."

"Good for you. Enjoy it while you can. Once the clients are on board, you won't be able to hang around up there. You'll be getting cozy with the rest of us in the trenches."

I get a sinking sensation in the pit of my stomach just thinking about spending the next three months locked away in a tiny, airless room in the bow of a ship. But I hide that beneath the small, placid smile that I've learned to permanently affix to my face.

"Oh. Okay."

"Unless they're off the ship in port."

"Okay."

"Or unless you're requested by one of them. They get whatever they want, of course, even if it's the company of a particular employee for the night."

"For the night?" A tiny niggle of alarm sweeps through me. Surely that doesn't mean what it sounds like it means.

"Well, for the evening. Anything beyond that is a...personal decision, not a work requirement."

"Oh. Okay," I say a third time, slowly exhaling my relief.

"But you made one too many lefts. You should've taken a left-right-left coming out of your room, not a left-left-left."

"So I should go back down the stairs and —"

"Girl, that's too much trouble. Just go out that door," he says, pointing to a larger door across the room from where we stand, "and you're in the bar. There will be exits leading to the deck on your left."

I nod my thanks and make my way outside, even more determined to enjoy the experience and the scenery since it might be my only chance for a while. I've never been on a cruise, or on a boat at all actually, so this is a first — but hopefully not a last — for me.

I walk to the furthest point on the bow of the ship and lean into the V of the railing. The wind is warm and brisk, the sun shines on my face as it sets and all I can hear is the spraying sound of the wake as the boat cuts through the water. When I turn my head and look far to the left and scan the horizon all the way around to my right, I'm floored by how small and insignificant I feel. As far as I can see, there is nothing visible but miles and miles of ocean. It's both humbling and breathtaking. And maybe a little bit intimidating.

I lean over the rail a bit to look down at the front of the yacht where it stands still so far above the surface of the water. That's when I see them.

I gasp. Six dolphins jump and play in the water just ahead of the ship, as if daring the boat to touch them, but the boat dares not.

The orange light bounces off their pale gray bodies, glistening brightly as they make their brave arc in front of the yacht. With their mouths open as they squeak to one another, it looks like they're smiling at me as they breach the water for an instant and then disappear two seconds later. I'm barely aware of the delighted laugh that bubbles up in my chest and spills from my lips.

"Amazing, aren't they?" a deep, familiar voice says at my ear. Immediately, I stiffen, the smile dying from my lips and my heart doubling its beats per minute.

I turn my head to find Reese nearly pressed to my back. In the dying sun, golden highlights shine in his hair and his eyes sparkle like aquamarines of the highest quality. For a moment, I'm tempted to count every inky lash that rims his exotic eyes, but the flash of his brilliant smile takes my breath away and reminds me that I'm playing with fire of the most dangerous kind. I can't lean away; there's nowhere to go. My only option is to ignore him and return my attention to the view I was enjoying.

But there's no ignoring Reese when he wants to be noticed. He leans into me ever-so-slightly, imprinting the firm muscles of his chest, the flat plane of his belly and the hard length of his thighs on every surface of my back side that he touches.

"*This* is the most incredible view in the entire world," he whispers, his inflection matching the pressure of his body, making me think he's referring to me rather than the natural wonders surrounding us.

"I'm sure you're accustomed to beautiful scenery like this."

"I've seen some of God's most stunning creations, but this one has always been special to me."

I don't dare let him lull me with his charming ways. That ended badly once and he still has yet to even explain it, much less apologize for it.

Not that there's anything he could say to make what happened okay.

My thoughts trigger a burst of anger. I spin inside his arms, pushing away from the rail until he gives and steps back. "Well, this is a first for me, so I'd like to enjoy it while I'm allowed up here, if you don't mind."

With that, I march right back the way I came, circling to the other end of the deck rather than going back inside. I half expect Reese to follow me, but the next voice I hear belongs to Sig.

"I don't know what's more beautiful—this view or you."

I turn to find him standing behind me, hands in the pockets of his black slacks, dark hair blowing in the breeze. His grin is as playful and light as ever, immediately putting me as ease.

"Wow, you get many girls with lines like that?" I ask with a smile of my own.

"This is the first chance I've had to try that one out. How's it working so far?"

I hold out my hand and see-saw it back and forth. "Meh."

"Then tell me, O Aloof One, how does a guy like me impress a woman like you?"

"Why would you want to?"

"Because you're gorgeous and mysterious and you dance like you're dancing just for me. You fascinate me. Do I need to go on?"

I'm very flattered and I don't really know what to say, but, as usual, the stand-offish Kennedy who learned to function in self-preservation mode from a very early age rises up. "I dance like that for everyone. It's my job."

Rather than being offended or acting like a typical man with wounded pride, Sig grins. "Hell, I know that, but you don't have to ruin it for me. I'm a man. A big one. With a big ego. Let me think it's all for me, woman," he teases.

I laugh. "Fine, fine. It was all for you."

He nods and grins at me. "That's a little more like it."

Sig moves in closer to me, staring down into my eyes for a few seconds before he turns to stand at my side, offering me his arm. "Shall we?"

With an exaggerated shake of my head and roll of my eyes, I curl my hand under his elbow and let him lead me through another door that empties into the rotunda and main dining area. The first thing I see when I step over the threshold is Reese, standing at the other end of the room, talking with Brian and glaring at me.

Even in his aggravation, just the sight of him is enough to make my stomach flip over. He's so gorgeous, still so much the guy who turned my heart and my world upside down—dark hair that curls just a little around his collar, glittering eyes that see right through me, a jaw that makes my fingers itch to stroke it. And his lips...I've always thought Reese's mouth was the most perfect God ever created. Turns out it's part angelic, part evil. The evil part being the one that made me promises that he never intended to keep, of course.

As always when I get enthralled with the Reese that I loved so long ago, the hurt girl resurfaces to prevent me from making the same mistake twice. It's her that gives him a frosty smile and turns her attention to Sig at my side. My grin gets deeper and more genuine, however, when, from the corner of my eye, I see Reese's expression turn thunderous.

It makes me want to giggle.

Take that, *you egomaniac!*

My mood going into the dining room is generally lighter, even more so when I realize there are no seat assignments and I can sit wherever I want, which just so happens to be sandwiched between Sloane, who I really like, and Sig, who evidently really likes me.

The meal is delicious and the company delightful. Although Reese responds to comments and comports himself in a polite enough way, I can practically feel the tension humming just beneath his unaffected façade. As much as I hate to admit it, it thrills me.

He's made it known that he wants me, that he intends to have me. And I have made it known that I intend to make sure that doesn't happen. We are admittedly engaged in a battle of wills. But something deep inside me realizes that this is only the beginning, that Reese has yet to really even exert himself, and that when he does, this battle is going to become much more difficult for me. And much more dangerous.

But that's partly what makes it so thrilling. Somewhere in the back of my mind and the bottom of my heart, I wonder if I'm really strong enough to resist. Or if I even really want to. I wonder if there's a part of me that wants to get back what we had all those years ago, when love was still young and fresh and perfect and unscathed, to get that back even for a moment. Or a month. Or a summer. If that would even be possible.

On one level, I seriously doubt it. But on another level, I believe I'm strong enough to test those waters without crumbling into a thousand pieces when things don't work out. I've already given Reese those tender parts of myself. What's left now is harder, harsher. Stronger.

It's the rise of one dark brow that jolts me from my silent reverie. Reese is watching me. And I, lost in thought, have obviously been watching him.

Hurriedly, I turn my attention to Sig at my side, laughing at whatever he's laughing at, but having no clue what we're even talking about. Without looking back at him, I can almost feel Reese's amusement. His amusement and his predatory eyes.

CHAPTER SEVENTEEN

REESE

I've kept a loose eye on Kennedy the entire evening. I've watched her flirt with Sig. I've watched her interact with Sloane and Hemi. I've watched her try her damnedest not to look at me and try her best to ignore me.

And, best of all, I've watched her fail.

I've seen the little glances my way. I've observed the way she tucks her hair behind her ear when I speak and I've seen the way she smoothes the chills on her arms when our eyes meet. I can feel her attraction to me like the humidity in the air. It makes me want to strip her bare, to lay her on the table and lick the moisture from her skin while everyone else watches. And wants her. Yet can't have.

While it frustrates me that she's hell bent on resisting me, it also excites me to some degree. The feeling of conquest when she *does* give in—which she will, I have no question—will be even greater. And my baser instincts thrill at the notion of that.

So, in the end, I grit my teeth and bear it because I'm smart enough and strategic enough to let her have this time before I really start working on her. I'm content to let her think she's winning. Until I'm ready to win. And then it's game over. Simple as that.

After a glass of brandy in the lounge, the excitement of the day starts to wear on everyone. One by one, they all start to make their excuses and head for bed, Kennedy included.

Of course, Sig offers to walk her to her cabin. It sets my teeth on edge, but I smile and nod my goodnight to them anyway. As I watch her walk out of the room, head high, shoulders square, Sig's hand on the small of her back, I get a pang of...something. Something I felt a long time ago...for a girl I met in the woods.

Several minutes after they're gone, minutes during which I can't get that gnawing sensation to leave my gut, I get up and make my way down the stairs and down the hall to the bow of the ship where Kennedy's room is.

As I walk, I find myself imagining Sig threading his fingers into Kennedy's hair, kissing those sexy-as-hell lips, pushing her back into the darkness of her room. My steps get heavier. I get angrier the closer I get to her closed door. My chest is tight and my pulse is pounding as my body prepares for me to beat the shit out of my brother's future in-law if he has made the grave mistake of being in Kennedy's room.

Bang, bang, bang, I thump on Kennedy's door. I'm aware of how furious and aggressive the knock sounds. When I left the lounge, this was not how I pictured things going, but damn if she hasn't managed to piss me off anyway.

When Kennedy answers the door, barely cracking it to peek out, I struggle to keep my sudden rage in check.

"Are you alone?" I ask gruffly.

Kennedy frowns. "Of course," she replies as if I'm being ridiculous. I don't let her see the way my lungs deflate as I release the breath I was holding.

"Can I come in?"

She eyes me suspiciously for a few seconds before she nods once and steps back to let me in.

In the low light, I can see that she's already changed clothes. Now she's wearing some tiny little cut-off sweat pants and a worn gray tee shirt that says *Exotique* across the front. It draws my eye to the lush curves underneath and I clench my fists to keep from pulling her into my arms and letting the feel of her skin soothe my irritation.

"What do you want, Reese?" she asks as she sits on the edge of her bed, crossing her arms over her chest.

As agitated as I am, I can still find room to tease her. "Now *that's* a loaded question if I've ever heard one."

She gives me a withering look, but I can tell by the way she's flicking her fingernails, something she did when we were younger when she got nervous, that she's not as immune to my presence as she'd have me think.

Her next words surprise me. "Why did you give me this room, Reese?"

"Why not?"

"Because no other room is this nice."

"You haven't seen the staterooms then."

"You know what I mean."

"Is it so wrong that I'd want you to be comfortable? To have a little extra space and a window?"

"It is if you're expecting something in return."

"I told you what I want, Kennedy."

"And I told you that it's not going to happen."

I can tell my smile surprises her. "God, I love how feisty you are. You've changed a lot, haven't you?"

She raises her chin a notch. "I've had to."

I can't keep myself from moving closer. I don't want to. Waiting one second longer to put my hands on her is just too much. I have to touch her.

Kennedy doesn't move until I stop right in front of her, my knees brushing hers where she sits on the bed. She tilts her head back to maintain contact, but otherwise, she doesn't move a muscle. I'm not even sure she's breathing. I'm not even sure *I'm* breathing.

I reach down and push one long, silky strand of hair over her shoulder, my fingertips grazing her neck. I feel her twitch, like she got a jolt of the electricity that seems to always be moving between us.

"But some things never change, do they?" I ask her softly, feeling more and more like that nineteen year old kid the longer I'm around her.

Kennedy's eyes freeze over. "That's where you're wrong. Everything changes, Reese. Everything."

I give her a wry smile. "You're probably right. But that doesn't mean everything changes for the worse. Some things only get better."

"But most don't."

"That's not true. And especially in our case."

"You can't know that."

"Yes, I can. You can try to pretend that you don't feel it, but I know you do. There's something between us, Kennedy. There always has been."

"You're mistaken," she says boldly, but I hear the tremor in her voice. I see the forced bravado in her eyes.

"I'm not. Never about this. About us. I know you think you should resist it, that this is a road you don't want to travel, but trust me, you would enjoy it."

"There's more to life than pleasure, Reese." Kennedy stands, her body sliding up against mine in a way that makes me ache to toss her onto the bed and tear her tattered little t-shirt off. "And I wouldn't trust you as far as I could pick you up and throw you."

"Maybe you will. If you'd just be a little more open to me, you'd see that I'm right."

"Maybe I don't want to."

"But you do. And you will. I'll prove it."

"Prove what?" she asks.

I don't answer her. I simply smile as I bend forward to brush her lips with mine. It's a small taste that only makes me want more. But the shiver I feel run through her at the contact makes it easier to pull away. It just reiterates what I already know in my gut—eventually she'll be mine. She'll come to me. And I'll be waiting.

"Here's your schedule. You might need it." I give her the piece of paper that I brought for her and I turn to go. I leave the room, leave her standing.

Leave her wanting.

CHAPTER EIGHTEEN

KENNEDY

"So are you gonna tell me what's going on with you and Prince Charming?" Brian doesn't even pause as he leans into my leg to stretch it.

"What are you talking about?"

He rolls his brown eyes at me. "Oh come on! You didn't think I'd notice?"

"Notice what?"

"The way he looks at you...and the way you try *not* to look at him. Girl, you don't have to play Snow White with me."

"I'm not playing anything with anybody."

"And why not? This is a fantasy cruise. Don't you want a little fantasy for yourself?"

"That's not a fantasy. That's a train wreck."

"Wow, you don't sound bitter at all," he mocks with a smile. "I take it you two knew each other before?"

I feel my guard come up, like it always does. "Something like that."

"Well, maybe that'll give you an advantage. You're sure going to need one. I've never seen that man not get what he wants. What *or who*."

I give Brian my brightest smile as he relaxes back and then leans into me again. "Well, maybe this'll be good for him."

"This oughtta be interesting," he replies. "And you know I'll want all the details."

"I'm not really a details person," I admit candidly. "Not that there will be any details to discuss."

"This is a long trip. And a small ship. You'll need a friend. Trust me."

I just smile, letting the conversation die. And just in time, too. Brian and I both look toward the door when we hear it open a few seconds later. Reese strides in, looking refreshed and gorgeous as ever in his snug white t-shirt and black shorts. I've never forgotten what great legs he has—muscular, tan, not too hairy.

He nods at Brian and shoots me that bone-melting smile of his. And, of course, my bones melt. Then I become irritated. I hate that I react to him the way I do, but try as I might, I can't seem to stop it.

With determination, I turn my attention back to Brian. "What were you saying?" I ask politely, keeping my eyes trained on his, even though it's all I can do not to watch Reese as he crosses the room behind him.

Brian chuckles. "Yeah, that's what I thought."

I give him a disdainful look and then we both laugh. For another hour, Brian stretches and works my muscles relentlessly, even more so than the personal trainer for *Exotique*. And for that hour, Reese watches. Every time I sneak a peek at him, his eyes are on us, burning a hot path over every inch of my body. And even though I'm not as overt, and even though I hate that I do it, I find myself watching Reese, too. I watch his muscles strain as he lifts and pushes and squeezes. I watch his golden skin shift as he moves. I watch his lips purse as he exhales. And, from the corner of mine, I watch his eyes devour me.

When it's finally time for Brian to cool me down, my heart is racing and the sheen of sweat on my brow has nothing to do with physical exertion. It's like I've spent the last hour being touched and caressed, being stripped bare and consumed by Reese.

All from across the room.

I'm ready to bolt and get away from him when Brian lets me go. I need space, distance. But I soon realize those are two things I'm not likely to get when I'm stuck on a yacht in the employ of Reese.

And when he makes no bones about wanting me in his arms.

Evidently Reese doesn't plan to give me much of a reprieve from him. I've just had a shower and am sitting down to some oatmeal in the crew kitchen area when Karesh enters. My lips are puckered and I'm blowing on a hot spoonful when he stops at the table.

"Are you finding everything you need, Ms. Moore?"

I give him a smile and a nod. "I am, thank you, Mr. Karesh," I say with the spoon hovering near my mouth.

"Don't let me stop you," he says, returning my smile. "I've just come by to tell you that your presence has been requested on the main deck for the day. A late breakfast will be served if you'd like something else to eat. Be sure to wear your swimsuit. You should have everything you need in your room, but if you find that's not the case, let me know immediately and I'll see to it that you have it within the hour."

I simply nod and smile again, my mind already racing over what this might mean for me.

Why am I being summoned? Who has requested my company? What's expected of me?

As though the questions are visible on my face, Karesh touches my shoulder in a comforting way. "Don't give it too much thought. Just go and have fun. This *is* a pleasure cruise after all."

With a pat-pat-pat on my shoulder, Karesh nods again before he turns to leave, as though his words explained everything rather than making it worse.

A *pleasure* cruise? For whom? Because I *know* he can't possibly mean for *me*. I'm here to work. Nothing more.

It's with growing unease that I dump out my uneaten oatmeal, wash the bowl and make my way back to my room to look through my overflowing closet. It's not until I open the built-in drawers at the bottom of the closet that I see, among other things, the bathing suits Reese has so generously provided. Of course, they're much nicer than the ones that I brought, although a couple are far more revealing than anything I'd ever be caught dead in. I touch the sequined and intricately-painted suits, debating on what to wear. My eyes keep returning to one with swirls of teal and blue, like a peacock's plumage. I take it out and flip through the closet, finding a sheer floral top and matching short sarong in shades of green and blue. I slip it on, noting the perfect fit before I pile my hair on top of my head and push my feet into jeweled green sandals. There were even sunglasses in one drawer, so I grab a pair and slide them into place. If nothing else they will hide my eyes from Reese.

I remember Brian's instructions on how to get outside from my room way up in the bow of the ship. Left-right-left. Sure enough, it takes me directly to the doors that lead to the top deck.

Reese is sitting at the covered bar area that sits behind the small pool and hot tub. At either end are bowls and platters, stacked and arranged and overflowing with food. Beside him is Hemi. Sloane and Sig are sitting at the other end.

He notices me the instant I step outside. He's wearing sunglasses as well, but I would swear that I could feel his eyes meet mine behind them. I watch him, admittedly feeling a little breathless when his lips curve into a smile and he rises and makes his way to me.

I can't help but admire him—again—as he walks in his lazy lion-like way. He's wearing swim trunks in aqua, two or three shades darker than his eyes, and a white shirt, unbuttoned to reveal his wide chest and rippling abdominals. His hair is mussed from the wind and his square jaw is covered in a day's worth of stubble. As amazing as he was as a young man, this Reese makes the younger one look pathetic. He is nothing short of physical perfection now.

With one big hand, Reese reaches for my fingers, bringing my knuckles to his lips. "You look beautiful," he says softly, his thumb rubbing rhythmically up into the web between my first and second finger. The action sends a little shiver rippling through me and I stiffen against it.

Reese smiles, a devilish smile that makes me wonder how he knows the way he affects me. Because he knows. I'm certain of it.

I tug my fingers from his and force a smile of my own. "So, why am I up here?"

"Because I want you up here."

"To do what?" I know it's a loaded question, but I want Reese to spell it out for me. It makes me feel better to be brazen and a bit difficult. It makes me feel strong and more in control to take the bull by the horns. So to speak.

"To keep me company."

"It looks like you've got plenty of company," I say, tipping my head to his family where they sit at the bar just over his shoulder, pretending not to watch us.

"But they're not the company that *I want*."

"Is this part of my job?"

"Your job is to entertain the people on this cruise. That includes me."

I search his eyes. He's enjoying this—having me at his beck and call. And although some part of me thrills at the idea, another part is shying away from him and the pain he once caused me. But I remind myself that this is the means to an end. What could be a *very good* end for me. With that in mind, I give him a bright smile.

"Then lead the way."

Reese makes no comment. He simply raises one brow and sweeps one arm toward the breakfast buffet set up at the bar. I take a deep breath and precede him, focusing on maintaining my smile in the face of curious looks from Sloane and Hemi, and a pleased one from Sig. But all the while, I can feel Reese's eyes on my back, warming me to my core.

****

All day, I've been treated like a princess. I've been waited on hand and foot, I've eaten some of the most amazing food imaginable, I've sipped some of the most delicious cocktails on the planet, all while listening to the Spencers and the Lockes tell stories about their life and their childhood. And through it all, Reese has never been far from my side.

He's barely let me out of his sight. He has lounged beside me on the deck, played beside me in the pool, soaked beside me in the hot tub and used every excuse under the sun to touch me. And every time he does, I get a little less immune to it.

Not that I was ever really immune to it. I'm just finding it easier to see the boy that I fell in love with in the eyes of the powerful man that he's become.

We just finished a light afternoon snack of fresh fruits and rich cheeses, accompanied by some sort of lemon and coconut drink that has my head spinning lightly. That coupled with the brightness and heat of the sun is making me feel sublimely happy and a little drowsy.

Groggily, I lift my head from the padded lounge chair when a shadow falls over me. It's Reese. He'd excused himself to go inside for a minute. And now he's back.

"If you're going to lie in the sun like that, you need some sunscreen. You're getting a little pink."

"Oh," I say, not too concerned. I'm dark complected, so I don't burn easily. "I'll put some on in a few minutes."

Without another word, Reese turns and walks back inside, returning a few seconds later with a white tube. "Here," he says, sitting on the edge of my chair at my waist, "let me."

It occurs to me that I should politely decline, but it's not a very persistent thought in the warm honey that my mind has become, so I dismiss it easily. I watch Reese flip open the cap and squeeze a glob of lotion onto his palm and then rub his hands together. When his skin makes contact with mine, I let the sigh in my chest escape in a light puff of air that the wind carries away.

I close my eyes, lulled by the deep rumble of Hemi's voice as he talks to his girlfriend and her brother, as Reese drags his fingers from my shoulder to my wrist, coating my arm in a rich layer of cream. I feel the tickle of his side against mine as he leans over me to give equal time to my right arm. After a short pause, during which I can hear him opening and closing the lotion tube, I feel his hand touch just below my throat as he rubs the scented balm into my skin.

Reese's palm strokes a slow path—much slower than the ones he made over my arms—from left to right across my chest. Back and forth, he inches his hand toward the top edge of my bikini. My breath hitches in my throat the closer he gets. Deliberately, he dips his fingers under the edge of the stretchy material and skims the tops of my breasts. My eyes pop open when I feel my nipples pucker into tight nubs.

I find Reese's eyes trained on me. He's not watching what he's doing or seeing how my body is reacting to him; he's watching me. He's observing my reaction in my face, in the tremble of my lips and the pink of my cheeks that I know is there.

Without taking his eyes off mine, Reese squeezes more lotion into his hand and sets his palm on my belly. Again, his fingers flirt with the edge of my suit, teasing the underside of my breasts and starting a throb between my legs. We watch each other as he makes his way down my stomach, his skin moving slickly over mine as he circles my navel.

His hand skates over the curve of my waist, down toward my back on each side before crossing my belly again and heading for the skimpy band of my bottoms. My muscles tighten when Reese turns his hand, fingers pointing down, and slips the tips under the material of my suit. I want to glance to my left to see if the others are watching us, but I can't pull my eyes away from the fiery grip of his blue-green ones. I know Reese's body hides part of mine from the view of the others and something about that makes my belly flutter with excitement.

I lick my dry lips when I see the knowledge in Reese's eyes. He knows that this is exciting me. He knows that *he* is exciting me.

"If we were alone, I'd put lotion on every silky inch of your skin," Reese whispers. I hear it like I have super hearing, like my ears are attuned to his voice above every other sound in the world. "Unless you'd like me to do it anyway. No matter who's watching."

A wicked light flickers in his eyes and, for the space of a single shaky breath, I consider letting him. But then my foggy mind registers the sudden absence of other voices and I realize that all other conversation has stopped.

With sheer force of will, I drag my eyes away from Reese's and glance at the trio sitting to my left. Hemi and Sloane are smiling and looking at one another. Sig is wide-eyed and focused on me.

"Damn, how'd I miss the sunscreen party? I'm next," he says with comical enthusiasm as he smacks his hands together and goes to rise from his chair. Hemi and Sloane laugh.

The moment is lost, so I wind my fingers around Reese's wide wrist and stop the movement of his hand. It's like grabbing a shaft of iron. I know that if Reese didn't want to stop, there's nothing I could do about it. And the firm set of his jaw confirms it. Yet he stops anyway, a show of respect for me and my wishes. I can see the regret in his expression, though, a sentiment that is reluctantly mirrored in my own. I make a mental note to watch how much I drink around Reese. Evidently, I can't afford to let my guard down for one second.

"You'll never get to dance for us if you're cooked to a crisp," Sig adds, drawing my eyes to him.

"We can't have that," Reese says, his gaze still locked on me. "Especially since she's dancing tonight."

Sig gives an excited whoop and I smile in his direction. I sit up and scoot away from Reese so that I can regain some kind of composure and clarity of thought. Even that doesn't completely alleviate the drugging affect he has on me.

"I didn't think we'd get entertainment since we aren't clients."

Reese answers Sig, but I can still feel that his eyes are on me. "Normally that's the case. Kennedy is the only dancer we have right now, but I'm sure she can give us a dance that will more than make up for the others."

"Hell yeah, she can," Sig agrees wholeheartedly.

I clear my throat. "Well, if that's the case, I guess I'd better get downstairs and start getting ready."

Reese puts out a hand to stop me. "I didn't say you were dancing *now*."

"But I need time to prepare," I tell him, pulling away.

"Not *that* long."

I move to stand, trying my best to shake off the disconcerting web he has somehow managed to weave around me. "This is my first dance here. I don't know where anything is at."

"I'll give you whatever you need," he replies softly.

"No, you stay with your guests. I'll call Karesh."

Before Reese can argue further, Sig interrupts. "Don't forget who you're dancing for tonight," he teases with a wink.

I can feel Reese's eyes on me as I answer him. "Oh, I won't."

As I make my way back to my room, I take the route I took the first time I left the crew quarters, which is by way of the kitchen. There are four people, all in hats and aprons, bustling about, probably getting dinner preparations under way. The guy I saw yesterday, the one I assumed was the chef with his taller-than-everyone-else's white hat perched atop his rusty-red head, glances up from some raw meat he's inspecting and smiles in my direction.

"May I help you?" he asks politely.

"I was just hoping to get a bottle of water to take back to my room. Between the sun and the drinks…" I shake my head as I let the sentence trail off. The chef wipes his hands and comes around to where I'm standing.

"You're Kennedy, right?" he asks, still smiling as he reaches me.

"I am," I answer, finding his light brown eyes friendly and warm. "I don't think we've met."

"We haven't, but Brian told me all about you. I'm Lee Howard, Head Chef. It's nice to meet you."

He extends his hand and I clasp it for a firm handshake. "It's nice to meet you, too, Lee."

He pulls me in to whisper conspiratorially from one corner of his mouth. "Technically all the crew is supposed to get their supplies from the kitchen in the bow, but those rosy cheeks are telling me you need the good stuff today."

"Oh, I'm sorry. I didn't...I just didn't even think about that..." Now I feel like an ass for stopping in here like I belong with the people up on deck rather than the worker bees below. I hold out my hand to stop Lee as he turns toward an enormous walk-in fridge. "I'll get something down there. I'm so sorry."

He waves me off, continuing on into the refrigerator. "No skin off my nose, Kennedy. Here," he says, handing me a brilliantly blue bottle of sparkling spring water that probably costs twenty dollars rather than the fifty-cent bottles of flat water that are probably stocked for the crew.

"No, I can't. Really. It wouldn't be right."

"Sweetie, enjoy it while you can." Lee pushes the water into my hand and turns me toward the exit that will take me to my room. "Come talk to me sometime. Any friend of Brian's is a friend of mine."

I glance over my shoulder to see him give me a smile and a wave before he heads back across the kitchen to return to checking his meat.

Checking his meat...that sounds bad, I think, snickering to myself as I crack open my bottle of water and wind through the halls toward my room.

Once inside the cool, dim interior of my quarters, I collapse on the bed and take a few more sips of water, enjoying the light spin of my head as I think back on the day.

Reese has been charming and attentive, flirtatious and sexy. He's treated me like precious glass all day. Just like the old Reese did.

I frown against the bitter thoughts that follow, thoughts of how that Reese was a figment of my imagination, of how that Reese up and left me without a word after all that happened. I'm teetering between the glow of pleasure and the gloom of memories when I hear a knock at my door. My heart lurches inside my chest and a little bubble tickles the pit of my stomach.

I bolt up off the bed and hurry to the door, pausing for a fraction of a second to take a deep breath and school my features before I open the door. I wouldn't want Reese to think I'm happy to see him.

But the person on the other side of the door isn't Reese. It's Karesh. I have to swallow my disappointment and hide it behind a courteous smile. "Hi, Karesh."

He nods. "Ms. Moore. May I come in?"

"Of course," I say, stepping back to allow him to enter. For a moment, my arm twitches as I consider hiding my bottle of expensive water. But it's too late. Karesh's eyes have already made note of it. Or at least that's what my prickly conscience is telling me.

"All the drinks and the sun today…" I tell him with a smile, tipping up the bottle as though I have no reason to hide it. Karesh simply smiles.

"I understand you'll be dancing tonight. If you have questions, please don't hesitate to ask."

"Oh," I tell him, feeling stupid over the water now. "Yes, of course. I think I can find everything I need."

"The showroom is directly below the lounge. You should be ready by nine."

"That shouldn't be a problem."

"If you'll let me know your music selection, I'll let Armand know. He's in charge of the sound system throughout the vessel."

"Okay. Ummm, I guess *Feelin' Good* by Michael Bublé if you have it."

"If not, he can get it. We can procure virtually anything you want or need. If not immediately, then within a day or two, depending on where we are in the ocean."

I nod. "I think I have everything I might need, but thank you."

"Yes, ma'am. Also," Karesh begins, clearing his throat. "Mr. Spencer wanted these delivered to you."

Karesh hands me a white envelope. I take it, curious as to what Reese might want me to have that comes in such a form. "Thank you."

Karesh nods again. "Also, he's requested you at dinner tonight."

Warm blood fills my face and gushes through my veins. It's pleasure, plain and simple. As much as I hate that it does, Reese's desire to have me around makes me happy.

"What time?" I ask, hoping Karesh can't see my pleased flush.

"Seven sharp."

I nod again.

"If you need anything, just remember I'm at 300 on the phone. Otherwise, I'll leave you to your preparations."

"Thank you."

It's Karesh's turn to nod again as he turns and leaves my room. He's so formal it makes me feel like white trash. Luckily, I grew up around the wealthy, so it's nothing new. And at least I know how to comport myself like I'm accustomed to it.

As soon as he has shut the door and I hear his light tread falling further and further from my room, I tear open the envelope and remove a single folded sheet of paper. Printed on it at the top is Reese's full name followed by a doctor's name and a lab service's name and address. Below that is a long patient number and then a list of tests on the left and results on the right.

My mouth falls open. They're all tests to check for STDs. They're all negative, which is great, but at the moment, I could care less. Fury heats my skin and floods my blood with adrenaline.

How dare he? How dare that presumptuous asshole have his lackey give me STD results as though me ending up in his bed is a foregone conclusion.

"Like hell I'll be at dinner tonight," I mutter as I stomp over to the phone beside my bed and angrily punch in a three followed by two zeroes.

A voice answers immediately. "Karesh."

"Hi, it's Kennedy. On second thought, I don't think I'll be able to make dinner tonight."

"Are you ill?" he asks.

I bite back a bitter laugh and refrain from giving him a very detailed explanation on just how "ill" I am. But Karesh doesn't mean ill as in angry; he means ill as in sick.

"No, but I had quite a bit to drink and I need to get it out of my system before the show."

While I'd love to give Karesh one heck of a message to deliver to Reese, I know that's not something that would ever get conveyed appropriately. No, that's something I'll have to tell him face to face. And, by the time I stew in this for the rest of the day, I'll be more than happy to do so tonight if he so much as looks at me the wrong way.

"Very well. I'll let Mr. Spencer know."

"Thank you."

If Reese wants a show tonight, I'll give him a show. A show for his guests. Just like I was hired to do. He'll see that I'm not his and that I never will be.

CHAPTER NINETEEN

REESE

It took every bit of willpower that I have not to go to Kennedy's room earlier. It's not often that I have to wait very long for something that I want. But Kennedy is different. We have history. A lot of history. And she's determined to let that be an issue. But as much as I don't like it and as hard as it is to go slow, I'm equally determined to do whatever is necessary to get her in my bed again. What began as a simple desire has blossomed into an obsession. She's under my skin, in my blood, and I won't be satisfied until I can feel her wanting me from the inside, tight and wet.

When nine o'clock finally rolls around and we are gathered in the show room, surrounded by crushed velvet covered walls and the deep thump of music, I'm so anxious I'm ready to snap.

With a casualness that belies my coiled insides, I stretch out my legs in front of me and sip my seventy-year-old scotch, my eyes glued to the curtain through which Kennedy should soon be emerging. When the lights dim further and the music fades, I feel like both holding my breath in anticipation and exhaling it in relief.

Michael Bublé's voice drifts from the speakers. We all fall quiet and watch, waiting for Kennedy to appear. Only she doesn't. He sings the first few lines and there's no sign of her. The curtain parts the slightest bit and a straight-backed chair glides smoothly across the polished floor of the stage, but still no Kennedy.

The singer's voice carries softly on, my anticipation rising with it. Then, just as the music starts up with a blare of horns, the curtain parts with a flourish and out struts Kennedy. She's wearing a hat again. A tall, black top hat set at a cocky angle that hides her face in shadow. It perfectly complements the tuxedo shirt and jacket that she's wearing.

Moving in time with the music, Kennedy walks past the chair, reaching behind her to drag it along with her as she moves closer to center stage. When the horns stop, Kennedy whips the chair around, raises one long leg and plants a high, high heel in the seat. She's wearing nothing from the waist down but shiny black panties that I get a glimpse of every now and again. I've never wanted to rip a tuxedo off someone before. But I do now. More than I would ever comfortably admit to.

Kennedy folds her upper body over her bent leg, trailing her fingertips from her ankle to the top of her thigh, pushing the tails of the tux back just enough to give me a gut-clenching glimpse of her deliciously-formed ass. She whirls again, turning to sit primly on the edge of the chair before leaning back and easing into the floor, her legs spreading into a perfect split before she reaches behind her and flips the chair over, setting it down in front of her.

For just over three minutes, I watch her work that chair. She reminds me of a cat rubbing its long, slender body in and around the legs, stretching over the back and winding around the seat. It isn't until her dance is nearly over that she rips her hat off, like I saw her do that night at *Exotique*, and throw it into the crowd.

Only this time she throws it to Sig.

Her hair floats around her face, but it doesn't conceal it, so I can plainly see the smile that she gives him. I can also plainly see the look that she gives him as she straddles the chair and arches her back. My blood goes from boiling to icy in those few seconds. I have to grit my teeth when I hear Sig say, "Come here and I'll help you with the rest of that outfit."

Kennedy grins at him, the tip of her tongue sneaking out at one corner of her mouth. For a few seconds, I think of standing up, taking my own chair in hand and swinging it right into Sig's face until I hear bone crunch. But I don't. God knows how, but I don't.

I'm fuming as Kennedy ends her dance and walks in that loose-limbed way she has off the stage and back through the curtain. I sit silently in my chair, listening to Hemi and Sloane as I seethe, thinking to myself that Sig will keep his mouth shut if he knows what's good for him.

"I wish I was sexy like that," Sloane says to Hemi, still talking about Kennedy's performance.

"You're the sexiest woman I've ever met, baby. If that had been you up there, dancing in half of a tuxedo, you'd be lying naked on that stage right now. Covered only by me."

"Good God! Will you two shut the hell up? I was having a damn fine time until my ears started to bleed," Sig complains.

When I can't stand it any longer, I jump up out of my seat and onto the stage before the next word is said. I stride across the shiny black surface and duck between the two halves of the heavy curtain in search of Kennedy. Only she isn't back stage. I stomp around for a minute, looking for her in all the logical places before I take off down the hall to the front of the boat where the crew quarters are located. When I reach her room, I'm still irate as I raise my fist to bang on her door.

CHAPTER TWENTY

KENNEDY

I consider not answering the first harsh thumping that I hear, but when the second round of knocks is enough to make the panel rattle on its hinges, I figure I'd better open it before he damages something. The last thing I need is to be blamed for Reese breaking down my flimsy cabin door.

I walk to the door and fling it open, ready to shoot fire at Reese. Right up until I see how irate he looks. That gives me pause.

Grabbing me by my upper arms, Reese hauls me up against his chest and walks me backward into my room, kicking the door shut behind him.

"What the hell was that all about?"

I refuse to shrink from his anger. Instead, I meet it with a calm, matter-of-fact attitude that I don't really feel, but am glad I could dredge up anyway.

"I danced. I entertained. Just like I was hired to do."

"I didn't hire you to flirt with every man on this ship," Reese spits furiously.

"I thought that was just part of my performance. Like cozying up to you today on deck."

I know my words strike a chord when I see his eyes flash with a dark light. "Well then I guess I'll just have to take full advantage of your employment then."

His quiet yet somehow even angrier voice triggers my own temper again. "Is that why you sent me those lab results? You think working for you should include sleeping with you? If that's the case, then you can just drop me off at the next port and I'll find my own way home."

"I had Karesh give those to you so that you'd feel comfortable about everything when the time comes. As for *when* you end up in my bed," he says with emphasis, "you can rest assured that it won't be because you're doing your job. You'll be there because you can't stand *not* to feel my hands on you. Because you can't stand *not* to have my mouth on you."

"You'll be waiting a long time then, because I'm just fine *without* either of those."

"Is that right?" Reese asks, a strange look on his face. It only takes me a few seconds to realize what it is. It's resolve. Reese thinks I'm challenging him. And I can tell by the set of his jaw that he's more than willing to accept.

His grip tightens around my arms and he swings me around and plasters me up against the door as his body crashes into mine. The action startles me, making me gasp. Reese takes full advantage of my open mouth, covering it with his own.

The instant his tongue touches mine, I lose all ability to think straight. All I can do is feel and taste and remember. The onslaught is so unexpected, so *familiar* that it takes my senses by storm.

The taste of him hasn't changed. The scent of him, that clean, manly smell, is still there under the hint of his expensive cologne. And the feel of him...God help me, I've never been able to forget the way his body feels against mine. Every hard plane, every rigid muscle is pressed into my soft flesh, warming it. Exciting it.

Reese turns his head to the side, deepening the kiss as he slides his fingers down my arms to intertwine them with mine and raise our clasped hands above my head on the door. He leans further into me, his erection digging into my belly. My head is spinning dizzily as he lowers our hands then releases mine so that he can push my tux jacket from my shoulders.

His lips and tongue dazzle me as his fingers work the tiny buttons of my shirt. I don't know when I drove my hands into his hair, but I'm suddenly aware of the silky, spiky feel of it, reminding me of passionate kisses just like this so long ago.

The first touch of Reese's hands against the bare skin of my abdomen nearly shakes me from my thrall, but then they're sliding around my waist, down to cup my butt and lift me off my feet. Automatically, my legs wind around him, giving us the perfect intimate contact. Reese moans into my mouth, sending a burst of electricity straight to my core.

Pleasure has taken over, pleasure at his kiss, at the little sounds he's making, at the way he feels against every surface of my body. My head falls back on my shoulders of its own volition, giving Reese full access to my throat. His lips sear a path from my ear to my collarbone and then I'm falling, falling, falling.

I feel the mattress at my back just as Reese parts my shirt and closes his mouth over my nipple. I feel the heat and the moisture of his tongue through the thin material of my bra and I cry out, clasping his head to me as he grinds his hips between my spread legs.

But then, as quickly as it began, it's over. Reese is lifting his head, staring down into my face. His breathing is as uneven as mine and his eyes are glistening pools in the gorgeous landscape of his face.

"I've never forgotten you, Kennedy. I've never stopped thinking about you, about us. I want you. And you know that. I promise you," he says, dipping his head to kiss my chin, "that I'll make you *want* to come to me." He flexes his hips as though thrusting into me even though there are clothes between us. "Just don't fight it too long."

Straightening his arms to lift his weight off me, Reese brushes his lips once over mine and once over my still-aching nipple. Then, easing off the bed, he walks across the floor and right out the door, closing it gently behind him.

****

Three days later, we have finally reached our first port—Hawaii. The whole ship is abuzz with excitement and activity.

For myself, I don't really know what to do. I haven't seen or heard from Reese this morning, so I'm not sure what my role is. Every other day, he's come to get me practically as soon as I wake up. He works out while I work out then he takes me up on deck with him for the day. Then, each evening, he comes to get me for dinner.

Until today.

I've seen no sign of him yet.

It annoys me that I'm disappointed, that I miss his early-morning visit. I tell myself that I've just come to expect it, but I know it's more than that. As promised, Reese is weaving a spell over me that's making me want to go to him more and more with every night that passes. He hasn't had me dance again since that one night when he came to my room afterward. When it's bedtime, I've lain awake every night, wondering if he'll come to me again, thinking of what I'll do if he does. Then, when he doesn't, I toss and turn until light dawns over the sea and he comes for me again in the morning.

Until today.

Just as I'm getting ready to head to my workout with Brian, there is a knock at my door. My smile is automatic. That is, until I open it and see Sloane standing where Reese should be.

Her mouth is turned down, her expression one of sadness.

"What's wrong?" I ask, a bit alarmed.

She reaches out and wraps her arms around me, pulling me to her and squeezing me tightly. "I just wish you were coming with us."

I grin, relieved and flattered. "I do, too, but I have to work, so…"

She leans back to look at me, the light of friendship gleaming in her eyes. "Well, I'm *sure* I'll be seeing you again." She gives me a wink and grabs my hand. "Come on. You have to say goodbye to Hemi and Sig. Otherwise, Sig will pout the *whole* rest of the trip."

I laugh, quickly pulling my door shut behind me as she drags me off down the hall. I liked Sloane from day one and I *really will* miss her on board.

When we reach the top of the stairs, I look out the window and see Reese walking away from Hemi and Sig. He must've been saying his own goodbyes. My eyes watch the spot where he disappeared as we make our way out into the sun, but there's no sign of his return. I try not to feel too disappointed by that.

Hemi is waiting for us with a smile when Sloane and I reach him. Sloane snuggles up under his arm, like she so often does, and turns her adoring eyes up to him as he speaks. "Sure you don't want to come with us?" he asks me. "I'm sure Sig wouldn't mind that one bit."

I glance at Sig who's shaking his head vigorously. "Not. One. Bit."

I grin. I can't help but like these people. "I guess I'd better stay on board. A girl's gotta work."

"And what fine work you do, if I might say so myself, Ms. Moore," Sig teases with a twirl of his imaginary mustache.

"I'll admit it's probably going to be all boring around here once you all leave."

I see the look Hemi and Sloane share. "Ummm, I don't think that's going to be a problem," Sloane says. "I think Reese will be keeping you *plenty* busy." She gives me an exaggerated wink and I laugh, dismissing her comment with a wave of my hand, but secretly thrilled by her speculation.

"Just be careful," Hemi says, less than playfully. "Reese is a pretty driven guy."

"I know. I've known that for a long time."

A strange silence falls between us until Sig pulls me in for a tight hug. "Anytime you feel like traveling south, you give me a call. I'll show you southern comfort like you've never even *dreamed* of!" he drawls, twitching his eyebrows up and down.

I lightly slap his arm and he releases me. I'm still shaking my head at his antics as the trio make their way off the yacht, leaving me at loose ends again until the clients arrive and somebody tells me what the hell I'm supposed to do with myself.

I make my way back to my room. I haven't been inside for five minutes before there's another knock at my door. Once again, my stomach lurches in anticipation, but this time I open the door to see Brian standing there.

"Welcome to play day in the woods, little red riding hood," he says with a broad smile.

"Huh?"

"Since we don't have clients until tonight, we get the day to explore a little. Do you have plans?"

"Ummm, not that I know of."

"Well then get your stuff. You're coming with me," he says enthusiastically. "There are a couple of places we love to visit on the island when we get the chance, but Lee can't come. So you're my companion for the day. Wear comfortable shoes and a bathing suit. And bring a hat. And a towel. I'll meet you up top in twenty minutes."

With that, he leans down and kisses my cheek before trotting off the way he'd come.

I'm thankful that Brian and I have fast become friends. I really like him. And even though I'm pleased that he'd ask me to accompany him and that he's sort of looking out for me, I'm still disappointed that I haven't heard from Reese.

As I pack a cross-body tote with the essentials, including a towel, I remind myself that this is Hawaii and that I don't need Reese to have a good time or to enjoy such a beautiful place. I'm still telling myself that as I head for the upper deck to meet Brian.

It turns out that *not* having fun with Brian is a practical impossibility. What started out as a bit of a down morning leads to a beautiful day in Hawaii. He first takes me to where a rented Jeep is waiting to carry us the few miles to a hiking path that leads to the top of Hualalai Volcano. Following that, we go shopping in Kailua Kona and then we take a short bike trip to a private beach beyond a thatch of forest near the coast. There, we swim in the most heavenly waters on earth.

As we splash around in the crystal clear Pacific, we chit chat about things that any friends might talk of, including our love lives.

"Yeah, Lee and I usually come here together. It's a great place to get a little alone time when clients or employers or other crew members aren't watching." He gives me a conspiratorial wink.

"So you and Lee are…are…"

"Lovers?" he asks with a grin. "Yes, you can say it."

"I didn't mean…I mean…I'm just not used to talking about this kind of thing with anybody."

"Don't you have girlfriends to talk to back home?"

I shrug, focusing on the flutter of my hands just beneath the glistening surface. "Not really. It's hard for me to get close to people."

"Well, then let's bond, girl," Brian says with a flourish. "Come on," he says, taking my hand and towing me back toward shore. "Let's get free."

"What's getting free?" I ask, pushing my legs through the water to keep up with him so that he doesn't actually start to drag me.

"That's when we strip down and get some sun *all over*."

I pull back against the grip he has on my hand. "You've got to be joking! I am *not* taking off my clothes in public."

Brian stops to give me a dubious look. "This is hardly public," he says, sweeping his hand across the empty, tree-lined beach.

"But still…"

"But nothing. You need to loosen up. And I'm just the person to help you do it."

"Not likely."

Brian stops again, frowning down at me. "What is it? Have you neglected your grooming? Are you hiding a Rapunzel-length braid down there somewhere?"

I can't help but grin at his offended expression. "You're sick, you know that? And what is it with you and fairy tale references?"

"Don't change the subject. Now you've got me curious. What are you hiding?"

"Nothing. God."

"Good. Then come on. Let's get naked."

He tugs me up to our towels and then releases my hand to start stripping. I watch his unabashed undressing, taking in his fantastic body. It quickly becomes obvious that he sunbathes in the nude quite often. There's not a white patch of skin anywhere on him.

"That's The Bishop," he says, catching me as I look him over.

My eyes fly to his and my lips quiver in amusement. "You call your…your…junk 'The Bishop'?"

"Hell yeah! If you had junk like that, wouldn't *you* give it an awesome name?"

I let my giggle go and admit to Brian, "Probably."

The smile he gives me is happy and relaxed. "Now, your turn."

As if he knows his attention might make me uncomfortable, Brian stretches out on his towel, tucks his folded hands behind his head and closes his eyes. I watch him for a few seconds, debating whether to run back to the water or just plop down on my towel, too.

"Just because my eyes are closed doesn't mean I don't know you're still wearing too many clothes," he says in a sing-song voice, making me roll my eyes. "And don't you roll those big green eyes at me."

That makes me laugh outright. "Are you sure your eyes are closed?"

"Just do it, for god's sake."

I exhale loudly. "Fine, but you better never tell a soul about this."

"I make no promises. I might have to sell your wares to the clients."

"The hell you will!" I exclaim, reaching for the ties to my top.

Brian laughs this time. "It's not like that. Unless you want it to be, of course."

"Which I don't," I assure him as I hurriedly drop my top then my bottoms and flop down on my towel.

"I doubt that would end well anyway."

"What's that supposed to mean?"

"I'd say our fearless leader would draw and quarter any such unlucky bastard and then toss his bits and pieces into the sea."

I turn my head to look at Brian. He squints his eyes and looks over at me, too.

"Why do you say that?"

"Girl, everybody knows he's got a thing for you."

"He does not."

Brian snorts. "Whatever you say."

When he closes his eyes and turns his face back up toward the sun, I nibble my lip for a minute before asking. "What makes you say that anyway?"

Brian's lips curve into a smile. "I know him. I've seen him around a lot of beautiful women and I know when he wants one of them. And trust me, that man wants you."

That's not quite the answer I was hoping for. "Well, he'd better get used to disappointment because he's not going to get me."

"Mmmm hmmm," Brian murmurs doubtfully. "By the way, nice rack."

I jerk my head back around to find Brian grinning broadly. I punch his rock-hard arm. "You weren't supposed to look."

"I had to make sure I didn't need to rent a bushwhacker while we were here."

"You're sick," I half laugh-half sneer.

We both fall quiet and I find the combination of easy companionship and warm sun a very effective muscle relaxer. It's not long before I feel like I might doze off. That's when I feel eyes on me. Like a little prickle along the nape of my neck. I cross my arms protectively over my chest as I sit up and look around. I don't see anyone else. It appears we are as alone as ever. But as I lie back on my towel, I wonder if there's any way Reese could have found us. Reflexively, my nipples furl into tight buds, thoughts of his mouth on me bringing about a very physical reaction.

That signified the end of any relaxation I might've had.

CHAPTER TWENTY-ONE

REESE

Whether they know that *I* know is debatable, but I'm aware of Brian's relationship with Lee. I'd have to be a complete fool not to notice. A man has a sixth sense about these things.

I've never said anything because it hasn't become a problem. And I hope it won't.

When I went to get Kennedy late this morning and she wasn't in her cabin, it didn't take much asking around to find out that she went ashore with Brian. Lee was more than happy to tell me where Brian took her. I don't know if Brian simply told him or if they have special places they go together when neither is working. Either way, I finally located her.

I heard talking and hushed laughter as I walked the shaded trail that led through the dense vegetation. I recognized the higher tones of Kennedy's voice so I knew I was on the right path. I expected to find her when I reached the end of the forest, but nothing could've prepared me for the sight of her lying naked on a white-sand beach, bathed in golden sunlight. Or the jealousy that streaked through me when I saw a man at her side.

The fact that Brian is gay makes no difference to me. I don't want any man enjoying Kennedy like this unless that man is me.

As I watch them, fuming and debating how to approach them, Kennedy grows still, her face going lax as though she might be falling asleep. I let my eyes roam her perfect form. High cheekbones turned up to the sun. Graceful arms tucked against her sides. Lush, round breasts standing firm in the center of her narrow chest. Flat stomach and gently flaring hips. Small triangle of short hair between her slim thighs. I've never wanted anything more than I want her right this minute. Not ever.

To touch her...to put my hands on her and my fingers inside her...to taste that creamy skin...to feel her liquid desire bathing my cock from deep inside...

I see her brow furrow before she moves her head. As though she can sense my eyes on her, she crosses her arms over her chest and sits up to look around. I can't see her eyes through the slits of her lids, but I imagine she's scanning the area for someone or something. When she seems satisfied that they are still alone, she relaxes again, letting her arm fall back to her side.

Saliva pours into my mouth when I think of sucking on one of those pink little nipples. As I watch, they pucker, making my cock jump inside my shorts.

I bite back a groan as I fight the urge to go to her, to lick her hot skin and suck the moisture from between her legs. But it wouldn't happen that way today. Not the way things are right now, and certainly not with Brian beside her.

Besides, I want her begging me for it. And that will happen soon enough. Sooner than she thinks.

CHAPTER TWENTY-TWO

KENNEDY

I'm pleasantly exhausted by the time Brian and I get back to the boat. A nasty storm rolled in, but we were due back to the boat anyway, so our day wasn't cut short at all.

I stretch out on my bed, not quite ready to let go of the boneless feeling that I've had since I catnapped on the beach, when someone flings open my door, bringing me to instant alertness.

Even in the dim light from my single small, high window, I can see how beautiful the woman standing in my doorway is. Her long, wavy hair is the color of cinnamon and frames the pale oval of her face. Her cupid's-bow mouth is currently forming a small O and I can plainly see her hourglass silhouette, set against the light in the hall behind her.

"Who are you?"

"I'm Kennedy," I answer, still recovering from my shock of being barged in upon.

"What are you doing here?"

"This is my room."

"Since when?"

"Since last week when we left Los Angeles."

"Oh, well there's obviously been some kind of mistake," she says, finally smiling. "I'll get it straightened out. No big deal."

"What kind of mistake?"

"This is my room. This is always my room."

"No one told me that. Karesh just said that this is where Reese wanted me, so…"

I can see one fiery eyebrow arch. "Reeeally?"

"Yes, but if this is your room then I'm sure they can put me elsewhere."

Just the thought of being stuck in one of those tiny shared rooms with no window is enough to cast a very dark shadow over what was a beautiful day. But it was never my intention to usurp anyone's place here. I was just doing as I was told.

"I don't mean to put you out, but this is the only room with a bigger bed and…well… Reese likes to come and visit me."

I can see her suggestive wink. My stomach turns accordingly.

"Oh. I see."

"Yeah…"

"Well, in that case, let me call Karesh and have him put me in another room. It won't take me long to get my things together."

"Okay," the girl says happily, rolling her suitcase into the room behind her. "I'm Amber by the way."

"It's nice to meet you, Amber," I say perfunctorily, trying to inject at least a smidgeon of sincerity into my voice, because I feel absolutely none. I cross the room in the wake of her trail of expensive perfume and pick up the phone to dial Karesh.

"What do you do onboard?" she asks as she leans her case up against the closet.

"I dance," I answer as I listen to the phone ring.

Amber opens the closet and I hear her gasp. "Are these yours?" she asks just as Karesh answers.

"Hi, Karesh. I'm sure you're busy right now, but is there any way you could find me another room? Evidently this one belongs to Amber."

"No, ma'am. Mr. Spencer wanted you there specifically."

I feel tears burn the backs of my eyes when I consider the reasoning that Amber gave me for why Reese puts *her* in this room. This was all just a part of his plan to sleep with me. That's it. Nothing more. There was no consideration for the fact that I might have some privacy or that I might have a window or that this room might be more comfortable. There was no special treatment because of what we shared so long ago. No, this was simply a maneuver of convenience on his part.

Well, I'll be damned if I'm going to be a foregone conclusion for him!

"Karesh, I'm not trying to be difficult, but if you don't move me then I'll have to find a place on my own."

"I'll speak with him again and let you know. Until then, stay put."

He hangs up before I can comment. I stare at the phone for a few seconds before hanging it up and turning back to Amber. She's still standing in front of the open closet with a slightly agitated look on her face.

"So you're the one."

"The one what?"

"You're the one he's going to favor next. He did this once before, but it didn't last long. I was back upstairs with him within a week."

I don't know if Amber is *trying* to twist the knife, but if she is, it's certainly working.

"Well, you needn't worry about me. I have no intentions of being the next girl in his parade of conquests." I pause, feeling guilty over how that must've sounded. "No offense."

"None taken. Reese is the kind of guy that's worth it. If you don't know that by now, you will. I'll tell you up front that I'm willing to fight for him, too."

"You won't have to. I have no interest in Reese. None whatsoever."

"Honey, that's what I thought at first, too. Most of us do. I graduated suma cum laude from Stanford and I come from good stock. Boston stock. I'm no dummy. I could make a very nice life for myself, *without* a man.

Even as a dancer. But when I met Reese...well, you know. He's the kind of guy that changes everything. I know he'll settle down one of these days and I damn sure want to be the one he settles down with."

"I wish you well, then," I tell her, fighting the urge to puke down the front of her beautiful violet dress. I walk past her, bending to take my suitcase from its little cubby at the end of the bed. I start opening drawers and haphazardly tossing clothes into my luggage. "I'll clear out the closet once I find another room."

"No rush. I'll come with you and we'll try to find an empty room. Maybe you won't have to share with anyone."

Amber gives me a warm smile and cleans out the last drawer for me, neatly stacking my shirts in one corner of my suitcase. I scoop my toiletries off the counter near the sink and dump them inside and zip the case. Amber grabs the handle and slides it into the floor. "Leave it here while we go look. You can come back for it. I'm supposed to be upstairs for dinner in an hour, but that'll still leave me plenty of time. And then I have to dance tonight."

My heart sinks even further when I hear this news. I haven't been summoned upstairs, nor have I been told I'm dancing. But then, considering her arrival, I'm not surprised. I offer her a shaky smile of gratitude. She returns it, loops her arm through mine like we are the best of friends and we set off to find me a new home.

CHAPTER TWENTY-THREE

REESE

Every minute that passes with no sign of Kennedy makes me angrier and angrier. I told Karesh to send her up for dinner, yet she hasn't shown. It's getting harder and harder to socialize with my guests and hide my increasing displeasure.

"Don't you agree, Reese?" Amber asks from across the table. I focus my attention on her, racking my brain for some clue as to what the conversation was about. She winks one blue-violet eye at me, her lips curving into a smile, but I don't appreciate it like I normally would. The only woman on my mind is Kennedy.

"Excuse me," I say, sliding back my chair and laying my napkin aside as I rise from the table.

I'm half way across the room when I feel a hand on my arm. I turn to find Amber has followed me.

"Not now, Amber," I pre-empt her.

"Are you looking for Kennedy?" she asks.

I feel the frown pull at my brow. "You've met her?"

"Yes, earlier."

I don't have to guess what that means. "What did you say to her?" My irritation rises. I know how catty women can be. I feel sure she put things in as unflattering a light as possible and that she is to blame for Kennedy's absence.

Amber raises her eyebrows at me. "She was in my room. She offered to find another one so I helped her. No harm, no foul. I didn't *say* anything to her."

"It's not your place to change cabin assignments," I bite testily.

"I can see that now. I thought there had been a misunderstanding. She was fine with it. It's not like I kicked her out."

"Oh I'm sure she was fine with it." My jaw aches from clenching my teeth so hard. "What room is she in?"

"Four. Right beside the kitchen. I tried to find her one she wouldn't have to share and you know everyone hates being right beside the kitchen."

"And of course that's where you put her." I squeeze my fingers into tight fists.

"It wasn't like that. I was trying to help her," Amber defends. "Go find her if you're so worried about her."

"That's exactly what I'm going to do. And from this point forward, you stay the hell away from her."

Amber stares at me for several seconds before she nods twice and, without another word, turns to walk away.

Furiously, I head for the stairs and, beyond them, the crew quarters. When I reach room four, the door is shut. I take a deep breath, doing my best to cool my temper before I break the damn door down with one swift kick.

I knock and wait for an answer, but I get none. That only makes me madder. I knock once more, but again there is no answer. "Kennedy, I know you're in there," I snap. I knock a third time, giving her one more chance. When she still doesn't answer, I twist the knob. It opens easily and I step inside, giving my eyes a moment to adjust before I let loose. But any angry words die on my tongue when I see Kennedy curled up on her side on the bottom of the bunk bed to the left. Her eyes are closed and, even in the low light, I can see that her brow is wrinkled and that there is an unnatural pallor to her skin.

I cross to her, hovering over her where she lies so eerily still on the bed. "Are you okay?" My voice is calm and cool, but my insides are knotted in anxiety. Is she sick? Is something wrong? She doesn't look well...

"Go away," comes her small voice.

"Kennedy, tell me what's wrong." I know my tone is sharper than what I intend, but I want answers.

"I think I'm seasick," she moans, still not opening her eyes.

I didn't even think that the onset of this storm and the rough seas that resulted would bother her. She didn't have any problems up until now. Of course, we've had smooth sailing until now, too.

"I'm sure we have something onboard that will help. I'll be right back."

I go in search of Karesh, who I find in the office, working. As usual.

"Don't we have something for motion sickness around here?"

"Yes, of course. Are you ill?" he asks, rising immediately.

"No, not me. Kennedy." My earlier pique returns. "Why didn't you tell me she was in a different room?"

"I didn't realize she had moved. I sent word to her room that she be on deck for dinner and Caesar said she agreed."

"Does Caesar even know what she looks like? Didn't he just board in Hawaii?"

"Yes, he did. I just assumed... My mistake, sir. It won't happen again."

I grit my teeth again. "See that it doesn't. But right now I need something to give her."

"I'll take care of it, sir. What room is she in?"

"Just tell me where it's at. I'll take it to her."

"Yes, sir," Karesh replies, crossing the room to unlock the second drawer in one of his three filing cabinets. Karesh is a man of many talents. He has a medical background, so he functions as our infirmary staff whenever needed until we can get help from the closest island.

He takes out a small box and removes an aluminum sleeve of pills to give to me. "She can take one every four to six hours. She might want to keep them on hand for when the sea gets rough. If she needs more, just let me know."

"Okay," I say, turning to leave.

"Again, sir, I apologize for the confusion."

"Just don't let it happen again. Kennedy is...she's...she's different. She's not like the others. And I don't want her treated like she is."

Karesh nods. "Yes, sir. Duly noted."

I make my way back to Kennedy, still fuming that she's in a different room. I stop by the crew kitchen to take a bottled water from the refrigerator. When I walk back into her cabin, it's empty.

I go back out into the hall, my testy temper flaring again as I contemplate where she might've gone. *Even sick* she's trying to get away from me!

But then I hear the door to one of the hall bathrooms open. I turn around just as Kennedy staggers out, nearly losing her balance as the ship dips. She leans up against the wall and closes her eyes, her face turning a pale shade of green.

"What the hell are you doing up?"

"I thought I was going to be sick again, but there's nothing left in my stomach. Just dry heaves."

I stuff the bottle of water in one jacket pocket and the pills in the other before I bend and sweep Kennedy up into my arms. I turn back toward her room, but I pause there, imagining her getting up and possibly falling on her way to the bathroom again. For that reason alone, I bypass it.

"Where are you going? That was my room?"

"Not tonight, it isn't."

"Reese, put me down. I can walk. And I can stay in my room."

"I'm sure you can," I say, tightening my grip on her.

"Reese, I'm serious. I don't need special treatment. I don't want it. I know why you're doing this and it won't work. I'm not going to sleep with you."

I stop in my tracks and look down into the now-dull pools of Kennedy's green eyes. "I'm not doing this so you'll sleep with me. But I'm not going to leave you down here when you're sick. Can't you just let me take care of you?"

"No."

"Why not?"

"Because I'm your employee. You wouldn't do this for the others, so I don't want you doing it for me."

I want to squeeze her and shake her and kiss her all at once. "You're more than just an employee to me, Kennedy. You're just going to have to get used to that."

"I'm sure Amber was at some point, too, wasn't she?"

The ship lurches again. Out of habit, I brace my legs to steady myself. Kennedy turns her face into my chest and makes a gurgling sound. I hate seeing her this way. And I hate that she doesn't want me to take care of her. But I hate it even more that she thinks she means the same thing to me that Amber does. Or ever did.

I pull her in closer and carry her in silence to other end of the yacht. I know she would never agree to stay in my room for the night, so I stop just short of my door, at the empty stateroom beside mine. Karesh knows that when I'm onboard, that room is to stay empty. I don't like having anyone sleeping beside me. Not even the women I'm having sex with.

But tonight I can make an exception. For Kennedy. Because I want her close. For her comfort and mine. I want to be able to keep an eye on her.

I open the door and carry her to the bed, laying her gently on the cream colored duvet. Immediately, she turns onto her side, curling into the fetal position.

"Here," I say, taking the water and pills from my pockets. "These should help."

I unscrew the cap on the water and punch one pill through the silver packet before handing them both to her. She takes them, pops the pill in her mouth and chases it with a gulp of water. She shivers and hands me the bottle. "Thank you."

"You should be feeling better soon."

I set the water on the bedside table. Neither of us says anything for a few minutes.

"You don't have to stay, Reese. I'll be fine."

"I won't leave until I know you're okay."

"I'm already okay. I'm just a little seasick."

"Regardless, I'm staying."

I hear her sigh, but she doesn't argue. I walk to the chair that occupies one corner and I sit down, watching Kennedy's face slowly relax as her breathing deepens. I feel helpless, but I know I've done the only thing that can be done for motion sickness. She's right. I really could probably leave and she'd be fine. The problem is that I don't want to. And for me, that really *is* a problem.

CHAPTER TWENTY-FOUR

KENNEDY

I feel drugged when I crack my eyelids to look around. Something is shaking my shoulder. Gently.

It's Reese, speaking to me, urging me to take another pill with a sip of water. Dizzily, I comply and then lay my head back down. Sleep comes quickly.

Some unknown amount of time later, I stir again, groggy and confused. I see Reese watching me from the chair. A million things go through my head and through my heart, but I don't want to think about any of them. I don't have the energy.

Comforted that I'm being cared for, that Reese is close and not upstairs or down the hall with Amber, I relax and go right back to sleep.

****

I'm awake again. I don't know how much time has passed. My head feels heavy and my vision is fuzzy, but at least the room seems a bit more stable. That or my stomach has learned not to care.

I know exactly where I am. And that the chair Reese was sitting in when I drifted off the last time is now empty. I'm both relieved and disappointed, if that's even possible. He said he'd stay. I'm relieved that he didn't because it's totally humiliating to have *anyone* see me this way, much less someone I'm trying to remind that I'm stronger than he might recall. But at the same time, I'm disappointed. His quick retreat simply tells me that Reese is every bit the liar that I've always known him to be, and that he doesn't even care enough about me to tell me the truth when I'm sick, much less when I'm well.

I reach for the bottle of water, taking a big swig to rinse my mouth before swallowing. Then gingerly, taking great care to move slowly in case that horrific nausea hasn't completely abated, I roll onto my back. I can't help but notice how much more plush and comfortable this mattress is when compared to the ones in the crew cabins. And how much warmer.

In the blink of an eye, I realize that the toasty temperature doesn't arise from beneath me, but from *beside* me. I turn my head just enough to see that Reese is lying to my right, his breath tickling my cheek and his body heat radiating toward me like a furnace. As much as I try to steel myself against the pleasure of finding him here, it's useless. My heart melts a little anyway.

He stayed.

Just like he said he would.

His eyes are closed and his breathing is deep and even. Normally those aqua orbs feel like my undoing. I can't risk looking at him for very long. But now, with Reese relaxed in sleep, I can study him as much as I want.

And I want.

He looks more like the boy I used to know when he's like this. Softer. Sweeter. Falling in love with nineteen year old Reese was effortless. On top of being drop dead gorgeous, even if in a more boyish way, he was strong and smart and funny, and he treated me like I wasn't the adopted foster child of the help. For those few weeks that summer so long ago, I was just a girl and he was just a boy. Two people who met in the woods to escape their respective worlds and find solace in each other's company then, eventually, in each other's arms.

I inch my way a little closer to Reese's warmth and close my eyes, letting my mind wander back to the last time I saw him in childhood. Back when I didn't know that there was *no one* I could trust.

****

Summer, 14 years ago

I push back the last pine limb that hangs between me and the clearing, catching and holding my breath as I move it. It leaves my lungs in a long hiss like a deflated balloon when I see that the meadow before me is empty. The lush, dappled grass is here. The tiny purple flowers are here. The heavenly quiet is even here. Everything is as it should be, only I'm alone. There is no Reese awaiting me.

I step into the opening, biting my trembling lip as I remind myself that I knew there was a chance he wouldn't show. I knew Reese's father was here and I knew he was afraid of what that meant for him and his future, but he promised me that he'd come, that nothing and no one would keep him from me. And I believed him.

Dejected, I walk around the little hidden clearing, mourning each tiny flower that I crush under my foot. Each one feels like a broken dream, a broken promise. A broken heart.

The snap of a twig draws my attention. I cock my head to listen. No one has ever accidentally stumbled upon this haven before. I say a silent prayer that this won't be the first time.

Another twig snaps and I hear the rustle of leaves crunching and limbs moving. Someone is definitely coming.

I hold my breath and watch in the general direction from which the sound seems to arise. My heart is a swollen ball inside my chest, filled with the sudden hope that it might still be Reese.

And then he steps into the meadow, the sun sparkling in the dark golden highlights of his hair, streaks that he's earned while working outdoors here at

Bellano with his uncle. His stunning blue-green eyes crinkle at the edges when he smiles at me and, as always, my heart melts.

"You came," he says simply.

"I told you I would. I thought maybe you..."

Reese's footsteps are muted by the thick grass as he crosses the tiny field to me. "I told you nothing would keep me from you."

"I know you did, but I knew your dad was here."

"He still hasn't arrived. Malcolm says he's supposed to be getting in this afternoon."

"So this might be our last day together?" I feel panic clawing at my chest. Reese is the one thing that I look forward to every day, the one saving grace this life has for me. Without him, the world is an ocean of despair intent on drowning me. He's like my life preserver, the one thing I can cling to that doesn't threaten to drag me under.

"No. Kennedy, I told you—"

"I know what you told me, but I'm just so afraid..."

"Don't be. He can't *make* me do anything I don't want to do. And I told you that if I leave here, I'm taking you with me."

"But it'll be three more years before I can leave with you. Hank would never let me go before I'm eighteen."

"Then I'll make him."

We both know that as powerful as Reese's family name is, there is no way he could *make* Hank give me up. Even Reese can't save me from some things. But I don't even want to think about that right now. I give

Reese my bravest smile and nod, unwilling to waste one more minute on such an unpleasant topic.

Suddenly, I feel frantic. I feel an urgency, a soul-deep need to share everything I can with Reese *now*, before life swallows up the last bit of happiness that I have.

"Reese, there's something I want to give you today."

"What's that?" he asks, brushing my bangs out of my eyes as he so often does.

I don't answer him. I just look up into the eyes that I've come to love so much and I pour out my heart.

He watches me for several long seconds, waiting for me to answer. When I don't, his smile slowly dies and he reaches up to cup my face. I know the instant he realizes what I mean. His eyes darken and take on a sort of...hungry look that makes my stomach feel like liquid fire.

"Are you sure?" he whispers hesitantly, as though he's nearly afraid of what my answer might be.

"Yes."

He bends his head, his lips brushing mine in a kiss so tender it makes me want to cry. When he starts to pull away, I rise up on my tiptoes and press my mouth harder onto his, winding my arms around his neck and holding on tight.

Reese slips his tongue between my lips and I lean into him, molding my young body to his bigger, firmer one. His broad palms skate down my sides, leaving a chill in their wake. Suddenly, I can't get close enough. I can't warm enough. I can't get enough of Reese.

With trembling, frenzied fingers, I reach for the hem of his shirt and slide my hands underneath, reveling in the hot smooth skin of his rock hard abdomen and muscular chest. Reese moans and moves his hands around to my butt, pulling my hips into his, thrilling me with the rigid bulge there.

"Make love to me, Reese," I pant desperately, urging him to pull his shirt over his head.

He leans back enough to do just that, tossing it somewhere on the ground behind him before his lips return to mine and he meets my passion with a blazing fire of his own.

In the quiet of the meadow, in the still of one summer afternoon, Reese undresses me and lays me gently on a bed of thick grass. He nuzzles my throat and kisses my chest. He laves my nipples and squeezes my hips, worshiping every inch of me until I'm nearly overwhelmed with the need to have his body covering mine.

I'm on the verge of visceral chaos when Reese leans back and digs a foil package out of his wallet before stepping out of his shorts. He stands naked before me, all tan skin and lean muscles. I watch his biceps shift and his abdomen twitch as he tears open the packet with his teeth and unrolls it over his enormous length.

As much as I want to squeeze my eyes shut against the thought of that fitting inside me, I don't. I don't want to miss one moment, one glance. I don't want to miss the sight of one expression as it flits over his face.

When Reese returns to me, covering my body with his, he rests most of his weight on his forearms so that he can stare down into my eyes. Time passes—a fraction of a second or an eternity. It could easily be either one. Finally, he speaks.

"I've never met anyone like you. And whatever happens, I'll never forget this perfect day, this perfect summer."

I bury my face against his chest as Reese eases into me. He strokes my hair and whispers soothing things into my ear until the pain passes. I let him think I'm reacting to the sharp sting of his body piercing mine, but I'm not. It's overshadowed by the agony I feel in my heart. Somewhere deep down, I know I'll never see Reese again. As much as he might want to save me, he won't. He can't. He's not strong enough. And I think he knows it.

CHAPTER TWENTY-FIVE

REESE

Someone crying my name—literally crying—wakes me from my sleep. It takes me only a split second to realize where I am and who I'm with.

It's Kennedy who is crying.

For me.

"Reese," she wails again, her face contorted and a single tear slipping from the corner of her eye to travel down her smooth cheek.

"I'm here," I tell her, drawing her into my arms. The agony in her voice is like a kick to the gut.

She buries her face against my chest, reminding me of that summer all those years ago. She did the same thing in the moments when she gave me her virginity, shedding her tears in absolute silence.

I cup the back of her head and hold her to me, dragging my lips over her apple-scented hair until she calms down. I know the instant she comes fully awake. She stiffens against me.

After a few seconds, I feel Kennedy's hand come to the center of my chest and push. I release her, leaning back until I can peer down into her face.

"Are you okay?" I ask.

"I'm fine," she answers casually. "Why?"

"You were crying and you said my name a couple of times."

I see color bloom in her cheeks, a nice change from how peaked she was when I brought her here earlier.

"Oh. Sorry."

"What were you dreaming about?" Kennedy lowers her eyes and I know by her hesitation that she's going to tell me a lie. "Tell me the truth. Please."

She glances back up at me, her eyebrows drawing together. "Why? Why does it matter?"

That's an excellent question. But I have no answer. I don't know why it matters; I only know that it does. "I need to know."

Her guard, usually so ready and so solid, isn't in place as firmly as it has been. I can see a softness in her eyes that isn't often there. Maybe it's because she's still waking up. Maybe it's because she's been sick. Maybe it's because I took care of her. Or maybe it's none of that. Whatever the reason, her guard is down and I plan to take full advantage of it.

I raise my hand to brush the hair away from her cheek, just like I used to brush her bangs back all those summers ago. I see the recognition in her eyes.

"I was dreaming about that day in the woods."

"Then why were you crying?"

"Because I knew I'd never see you again."

"I never meant to hurt you, Kennedy. I was just a stupid kid."

She nods and tries to smile. "I know. I had just hoped you'd be more." She sighs and I can tell she's preparing to move, but I'm not ready for this to be over yet.

"I thought about you for years after I left." She watches me intently, making no comment. "In a way, I wished you'd given your virginity to someone else. Someone who deserved it."

Her laugh is soft yet tinged with bitterness. "I wanted you to have it. It was the one thing of *mine* that I had left, the one thing I could give away. Before he took that, too."

I have an immediate reaction to what it *sounds* like she might've meant by that. The blood leaves my face and my jaw gets tight. But surely she couldn't be saying... "What do you mean?"

Kennedy's face is open and sad, not guarded and tough like it has been since the moment I saw her again. "After Hillary died, Hank started...visiting me. At night. In my room. He's why I would run and hide in the woods."

The bottom drops out of my stomach. "Are you saying that he...he..."

I feel like the world is perched, perfectly still, on a pinhead, waiting for her to answer me. I pray to God that I'm hearing that wrong, but something tells me I'm not.

"That's the one part of my innocence that he was afraid to touch. There would be proof. But that was the only part."

I'm filled with a mixture of rage and disgust for what Kennedy's father had done to her. It churns in my gut and burns through my veins. But I also feel an overwhelming sense of guilt. Kennedy needed a decent person in her life, not another shitty man who would ultimately hurt her in another way.

She looks down at my shirt, fiddling with one of the buttons as she laughs, a hollow, heartbreaking sound. "Yeah, I used to think that you could save me from him. From life. From sadness and pain. But then I realized that no one could. That no one *would*. There was no Superman waiting to rescue me. I realized that if I was going to survive, I'd have to rescue myself. I couldn't wait around for anyone else to do it."

I release Kennedy and roll off the bed to my feet. I drag my fingers through my hair, feeling like I might burst into furious flames at any moment.

I pace the floor, at loose ends, not knowing what to do with my fists or my anger, not knowing how to deal with this new information. I'm so caught up in my own head, so deafened by the sound of my rapid pulse in my ears that I barely hear her quiet words when she speaks.

"I know. It's disgusting. I couldn't even go to his funeral, I felt so dirty."

"Disgusting? It's...it's..." Words escape me. Then a thought occurs to me and I whirl to face her. "Why didn't you tell me?"

Kennedy is sitting up in bed, her hair wild around her head, her eyes wide and tortured. "I didn't want you to feel differently about me. I was afraid of what you'd think."

Her words are like a battle axe to the chest. "What kind of a monster did you think I was?"

Her smile is small, but it is belied by the shimmer of tears in her big green eyes. "I didn't think you were a monster. I loved you. I didn't want you to know. It was as simple as that."

"But Kennedy, you'd been abused! If I'd known, I would've taken better care. I would've been gentler. I would've..."

"You *were* gentle. You *did* take care. There was nothing I would've wanted you to do differently. You were wonderful. It was everything I wanted it to be until..."

In my head, I finish her thought. "Right up until I disappeared."

I see the hurt before she drops her eyes to watch her hands where they're toying with the hem of her shirt. She doesn't have to confirm it. I know I'm right. And I honestly don't think I'd feel more like a monster if I'd killed somebody. I might as well have killed Kennedy. By leaving her, I sentenced her to a childhood where she was at the mercy of another kind of monster. And, without me, she had nowhere to run, no one to help her. She trusted me when she couldn't trust anyone else, gave me the only thing she had to give, and I shit all over it.

My throat feels tight as I try to explain, knowing that nothing I say will ever change what happened, ever make a bit of difference. But I'm desperate to make her see... "My father came to get me that night. He'd pulled some strings and gotten me into Oxford for the fall semester. Said I was the oldest, the one who had to carry on the family name, the one who had to provide security for my brothers. He said it was my last chance to make my mother proud. He knew that if nothing else he'd said would make me go, that would. He knew she hated me. Maybe he even knew why. But I know he knew I'd do anything to finally get just one little bit of love from her. Just the tiniest bit of approval." I turn to face Kennedy, sitting like a damaged angel in a bed of pain. "Not that any of that matters now. It doesn't change the fact that I was weak. I never wanted to grow up to be like my father and he knew it. But that manipulative bastard outsmarted me and I grew up just like him anyway."

"You're not like your father, Reese."

"How can you say that?" I ask in angry disbelief. "After the way I treated you, how can you say that? Look what I've become."

"You always treated me well, Reese. Like just a girl. A girl worth spending time with. But if *you* feel that way, if *you're* unhappy with what you've become then change it. You're the only one who can."

I feel fingers of hopelessness wrapping my soul in their icy grip. "I am what I am, Kennedy. Like it or not, this is it. This is who I turned out to be."

"Then be happy with that. Regret will eat you alive if you let it. The only choice we have is to do the best we can and move on."

"Is that what you did? You moved on? Learned to hate me?"

The thought of her hating me is appalling, but I know it's a very real possibility, just like I know that I can't change the past.

"I don't hate you, Reese."

"You should."

"No, I shouldn't. You're right. We were both just stupid kids. I expected you to be my hero, but that wasn't fair. I shouldn't have put that on you. I needed to learn to be my own hero, because in the end, people can only hurt you if you let them."

"So now you keep everyone at arm's length so they can't get close enough to hurt you."

"Don't judge, Reese. You do the same thing."

I don't answer her. Maybe she has a point.

The need to heal her, to make up for all the pain I caused her, to give her happiness in place of all the heartache wells in my chest like a hot spring. Maybe it's man's instinct to protect the weaker sex. Maybe it's the residue of the love I had for a girl a long time ago. Maybe it's something more. Who the hell knows? But it's there.

I have a few weeks to show her some goodness in life before we part ways, a few weeks to put to bed old flames. To exorcise old demons.

I walk to the side of the bed nearest her, stopping to stare down into the face that's even more beautiful than I remember. More beautiful than it was yesterday.

"Let me make it up to you."

She starts shaking her head immediately. "No, Reese. That's not what I wanted. That's not why I told you."

"I don't care. I want to. All you have to do is let me."

CHAPTER TWENTY-SIX

KENNEDY

A small part of my brain is wondering if this whole scenario is even real. I just spilled my guts to the guy who broke my heart and shattered my world all those years ago. And he just gave me a little peek into his. And now he's offering...what? I don't really know.

More importantly, I can't believe I'm considering it. But the truth is, I never stopped loving Reese. Like scars and bad memories, some things never go away.

"Even if I wanted to, I can't."

"Yes, you can," Reese insists, dropping down onto the bed beside me. "You can be with me. You can let me be with you. You can let me give you the happiness that you deserve."

My heart thrills at what he's suggesting, even though I know he doesn't have forever in mind. I'm not sure I'd trust him to give it to me at this point anyway. But he's offering me right now.

Only...

"Reese, I work for you. Can't you understand that it feels...dirty? Like I'm a...a...prostitute? Like you're paying me to..."

That heart-stopping smile that has haunted me for years spreads across his mouth, bearing the edges of his straight, white teeth. It's lopsided and sexy and it turns my stomach to mush.

"Oh, I won't be paying you for *that*. You'll be off the clock for anything more...intimate." As if he senses my hesitation, he adds, "*If* you decide that's what you want, that is."

He's already giving in a little. A day ago, he wouldn't have left it at *if*. He would've said *when*.

"But Reese—"

"But nothing," he interrupts urgently. "Please, Kennedy. Do this with me. Don't make me beg." His eyes search mine until a teasing light enters them again. "Unless that's what you're into."

I can't help but smile. "God! Reese!" I exclaim, slapping his arm. He flinches like I hit him with a taser.

"Okay, so you're into the rough stuff. I can do that, too."

I laugh outright this time, rolling my eyes at his melodrama.

"I don't know. I just..."

Reese takes my hand and brings it to his mouth, rubbing his lips across my knuckles as he watches me over the top of them. "Then let me show you. Just give me a chance. I can give you some of the best weeks of your life. Trust me."

It's my turn to flinch as he touches my one raw nerve. "I don't trust anybody."

"But you can trust me. I'm not the boy I once was, Kennedy. I'll give you nothing but the truth. Nothing."

I bite my lip nervously, one reservation still preventing me from diving headlong into everything that Reese is offering.

He must sense my reluctance. "What?" he asks. "What is it?"

"I don't want to be another of your cruise flings, Reese."

"You're not. You could never be."

I raise my eyes to meet his. "I don't believe you."

"Then do it anyway and let me prove it to you. You're nothing like them and nothing I've said or done should tell you otherwise."

"But Reese—"

"Look, you sleep on it. Just give me tomorrow. And by the end of the day, you won't even *want* to say 'no'."

I'm tired of arguing, tired of trying to fight it. Tired of trying to fight this, fight *him*. "Okay," I agree, relief loosening every taut muscle in my body. I don't think I was fully aware of how very hard it has been to feign indifference to Reese, to pretend that I want nothing to do with him.

His smile is brilliant and I have the sudden urge to reach over and drag him down on top of me.

Reese gives me some sort of pleased man-growl kind of thing as he leans in toward me. Slowly. Closer and closer. I don't move away. I just watch his luminous eyes draw near, letting myself get lost in them. For just a moment.

"God, I can't wait for morning," he says, his lips so close to mine, I can feel his warm breath fanning them. But Reese doesn't kiss me. As much as I want him to, he brushes his mouth over my cheek then nuzzles it before pulling away. "Get some sleep. Tomorrow's going to be a beautiful day."

I nod as Reese rises and walks toward the door. When he's half out in the hallway, he stops and looks back at me. He smiles again and winks before he disappears, closing the door behind him.

****

I'm awakened by the tickle of lips and the light scratch of short scruff as someone kisses the curve of my neck. The warmth that floods my body has nothing to do with the heat radiating from the hard, masculine form at my back.

I open my bleary eyes to glance at the bedside clock. Not even 6:00 AM yet. "Don't you sleep?"

"Not when this is waiting for me in the next room. Do you feel like working out?"

I take a moment to do a quick self-assessment. No nausea, no lightheadedness, and the boat seems to be more stable this morning. "Yeah, I think I do."

"Good," Reese says, biting my earlobe and then smacking my butt through the covers before he scoots off the bed. "I brought you some tantalizing clothes to wear. I'll give you a minute to change and then we'll go."

"Wait, I'll need some things from my room," I tell him, leaning up onto my elbow.

"I brought your toiletries. Anything else?" Reese looks awfully proud of himself.

"I...uh...I guess not."

"Five minutes," he says, opening the door. Before he exits, he glances back at me, his lagoon-colored eyes twinkling. "Unless you need some help getting dressed. In that case—"

"No, I don't," I tell him, trying not to smile. "I'll be out in five minutes."

I can hear his dejected sigh all the way across the room before he shuts the door, muttering, "I don't know why you'd turn down a perfectly good offer of help."

I shake my head as I crawl from the warmth of the plush duvet and head for the en-suite bathroom. My guts are a jittery mess knowing that Reese is waiting for me and that today he's going to be turning up the charm (and likely the heat) big time.

For one heartbeat, the bitter skeptic in me starts to speak up, but I smother her with my happiness until I don't hear her at all anymore. Five minutes later, I'm opening the stateroom door to find Reese leaning up against the wall, arms and ankles crossed, waiting for me.

His eyes rake me from head to toe, taking in the skintight leggings and snug cap-sleeved tee that he brought me. I stop and let him look his fill. Then, since I'm feeling happy and plucky, I decide to give him the same treatment.

I start at Reese's white sneakers, working my way up the loose black running pants that hang just right on his slim hips to the flat stomach that's so perfectly defined beneath his dark purple fitted tank top. His well-developed pecs are clearly discernible beneath the fabric, his wide shoulders and muscular arms left open to my roving gaze.

When I skim his tanned throat and reach his face, his expression has turned from playful to fiery. His eyes are dark and his jaw is clenched. "I should warn you," he says softly, pushing away from the wall and walking to within an inch of me. He stops, looming over me until I have to crane my neck to maintain eye contact. "If you do that again, I'll haul your perfect little ass back into that room and give you the spanking you deserve for teasing me like that. Got it?"

A thrill races along my nerve endings, bringing my skin to tingling life at his nearness. "Got it."

"Wanna try it again and see if I'm telling the truth?"

He leans in ever so slightly, his chest brushing mine, my nipples hardening in response. He's teasing me and, for some reason, it's making me feel light and playful rather than defensive. Light and playful *and daring*. I arch my back the tiniest bit, rubbing my breasts against him in an almost imperceptible way. In exotic dancing, I learned all sorts of subtle ways to move my body to titillate and entice. I've just never used them on a man up close before.

"Holy shit, woman. You didn't tell me you liked to play with fire," he growls.

"What would be the fun in warning you?" I ask with a grin.

"I'm gonna count to three. One...two..."

Before he can get to three, I slide out from between him and the wall and, with a tiny squeal, move quickly down the hall. When I glance back over my shoulder, his eyes are glued to my butt. Giving it an extra little swing, I turn my head and smile.

Reese might be right. This might be the best few weeks of my life.

Until it's over.

****

When we reach the gym, it's empty. "I guess we beat Brian this morning," I say as Reese opens the door for me.

"Nope. He won't be working you out anymore," he admits, making his way to the stereo to turn on the music.

"What? Why?"

He doesn't answer until he's finished and back standing right in front of me. "Because. I told him I'd do it."

"Do you even know what you're doing?" I ask, feeling the twitter of butterflies in my belly.

"I've watched every single thing he's done to you until I can't watch it one more time. I don't want to see any hands on you unless they're mine."

"Brian's hardly—" I stop myself before I accidentally spill Brian's secret.

"I don't care if he's gay or straight. I don't like it."

I have to hide my pleased smile. "Then you'd better make this worth my while," I taunt.

Reese says nothing, merely raises one dark brow as he takes my hand and leads me to the mats on the floor. "Let's start with stretching."

As I lie down on the floor at Reese's feet, the heavy, sensual thump of *Closer* by Nine Inch Nails drifts into the room, bouncing off the walls and enveloping me in the tension that buzzes between us. His eyes are locked on mine as he spreads his legs in front of me and takes my foot in his hand. Still watching me, he runs his palm up my calf to the back of my knee, bending it as he leans down and in toward me, pressing my thigh slowly toward my chest. He eases up and then leans in again, pushing a little harder and extending my stretch in a long, languorous pulse.

The words to the song are resonating in my head and Reese's touch is resonating through my body as he reaches down to spread his hands over my hips, stabilizing them as he tucks his shoulder under my knee and presses harder. I feel the sting of the stretch in my butt, but I feel the throb of something else more toward my center. The throb of something deeper. Something hotter.

"Can you feel that?" he asks, his voice a low rumble.

I'm practically panting already. "Yes. I can feel that perfectly."

"Mmmm, good. Let's do the other side." Reese releases my left leg and shifts to give the right the same treatment. When he eases in and gives me that first deep pulse, he grunts and warmth gushes through me.

As he nears the end of my right leg stretch, I feel my heart start to race. If he follows Brian's routine, I know what's coming next. Sure enough, Reese doesn't release my leg; he straightens it, running his palm down the inside of my thigh as he scoots into the center of my body to stretch my groin.

Automatically, I lift my other leg and Reese presses a hand to the low inside of it as well, pushing outward, causing my legs to fall out into a split. He leans in, using a small portion of his body weight to exert pressure. Reese runs his hands up the insides of my legs to my ankles to hold them out straight as he eases forward against me to keep my stretch.

Oh, god!

I curl my fingers into tight fists where they rest at my sides. I want to beg him to kiss me and touch me, but I won't. I squeeze my eyes shut, not because it hurts, but because I can feel his belly rubbing between my legs.

"Look at me," Reese commands gruffly.

I do as he asks. The expression on his face is a mirror, reflecting everything that I'm feeling on the inside.

"Reese…"

He leans in even closer, his body grazing the flattened V of my spread legs. I can barely hear him when he whispers, "Are your panties wet?"

"No," I say automatically.

"Liar," he says with a wicked gleam in his eye.

I say nothing. I don't know what to say, other than to beg him to put out the flames that are consuming me right now, which I won't do.

"If I pulled them down right now and put my fingers inside you, you'd come, wouldn't you?"

I can't deny it. I probably would.

"I could make you feel so good, Kennedy," he says, leaning further into me, "but I won't. I won't until you ask me to."

I want to scream and moan and beg, but I do none of that. I simply let his eyes eat me up from the inside and I hold my tongue, determined not to give in so easily. This has become more than just me resisting Reese; this has become a battle of wills. He wants to make me beg, but *I* want to make *him* work for it.

"Can you wait that long?" I ask, rotating my hips under him the tiniest bit.

I know he felt it. I hear the air hiss through his teeth. "I promised you the truth, and the truth is I don't know how long I can wait."

I smile. I can't help it. I love that he would admit that to me. "Then maybe just a little bit longer," I say, tugging my ankles free of his grasp to wrap them around his waist.

I grin at the look of shocked desire on his face. Maybe I really do like to play with fire.

Lightning fast, Reese reaches forward and grabs my wrists, hauling me up and into his arms. He wraps them around me, holding me close as he picks me up a few inches and then drops me back down on his very noticeable erection.

"I wouldn't wait too long. It could get ugly."

"Maybe I like ugly. Maybe that's what I'm into."

Leaning forward, Reese licks a path from the V of my shirt neck to my ear. "I'll give you anything you want. As often as you want it. Ugly, rough, the dirtiest things you can think of. I'd do it all for you, baby. I'd come all over you and then lick it off. On that sexy mouth, on those delectable nipples. In that beautiful ass. So far up inside you, it wouldn't come out for days."

Reese is slowly grinding my hips against his, whispering naughty things in my ear, setting my insides on fire. There's friction in all the right places — body and mind — winding me up tighter and tighter.

"Mmm, the things I'd do to you. The places I'd put my fingers, the way I'd slide them in and out. Fast and hard, then slow and easy." The movement of his body under mine is steadily increasing, making it harder and harder for me to hold out. "The things I'd taste with my tongue. Damn, I can just imagine how sweet and creamy you are, like vanilla. And what that tight little body would feel like wrapped around my cock. Hot. Slick. If I close my eyes I can imagine you sliding down over me right now. So wet. Kennedy?" he whispers.

"Huh?" I moan, my entire being focused on the place where he's rubbing against me.

"I can feel those soaked panties through our clothes. Because you're close, aren't you? So close. Maybe if I did this," he murmurs, reaching between us to scrub the backs of his fingers over my sensitive center, stroking exactly where I need him to, as though there is an X marked there that only he can see. "Let me have it, Kennedy," he whispers, his lips grazing my ear as he speaks. "I wanna watch you come."

With Reese's eyes riveted on my face, refusing to let me go as he pulses one knuckle against me, I feel my body spiraling out of control. Over and over, he moves his hand until...

Oh shit, oh shit, oh shit!

My muscles squeeze and I swallow a gulp of air, determined to hold back the sounds of my orgasm. I move against him, unable to remain still any longer. My breath stops and starts, stops and starts and I pant against his neck, my arms gripping his broad shoulders as he rubs me through each wave. As I make my way back down to earth, Reese slows his assault, massaging me gently until my breathing returns to normal.

"That's just a taste," he murmurs, leaning in to nuzzle my throat.

Oh my god, Reese just watched me have a fully-clothed orgasm in the floor of a gym.

I can feel my face burst into flames and I hide it in the curve of his shoulder. Reese leans back and reaches up to cup my face. It's hard to look him in the eye. "Don't hide that from me. Don't ever hide that from me."

In the sweetest of kisses, Reese covers my lips with his own for a few, too-brief seconds before he wraps his arms around me again and holds me against his chest.

After a few minutes, when my buttery bones have started to solidify once more, Reese pulls back again. "Bet Brian never gave you a work out like that before, did he?"

His eyes are sparkling with mischief and, yet again, I have to hold back a smile.

"Wouldn't you like to know?"

His eyes narrow and he smacks my butt. Hard. "What was that? I'm *sure* I didn't hear that right."

I give him my most innocent smile. "Nothing. I didn't say a single thing."

"That's what I thought," he says, kissing the end of my nose. "How about some breakfast? I'm starving."

"I just bet you are," I tease, planting my hands on his shoulders and standing, my legs only feeling slightly wobbly. "Come on, let's go feed the beast."

"Oh you already are," Reese says, reaching for my hand as we make our way from the gym. "Trust me."

CHAPTER TWENTY-SEVEN

REESE

As much as I would've liked to have a quiet, intimate breakfast in my room with Kennedy, I figured there was no reason to put myself through that. Her sassy little comments coupled with the images I kept getting of her naked, showering in the room right next door was more than enough to convince me to bring her up on deck for breakfast. In public.

I smile just thinking about her reaction when I escorted her back to the stateroom next to mine rather than her tiny shared room in crew quarters. "I had Karesh bring your things here."

She looked at me with worried eyes. "I don't want the others to think that I'm—"

"I don't care what the others think and neither should you. *I* want you here. *I* want you close to me. That's all that matters. Everyone else can go to hell."

She might've wanted to argue, but she didn't, especially when I opened the door to the stateroom and Karesh had made the few other changes I'd asked him to make. Fresh flowers were overflowing a crystal vase that he'd placed on the dresser. Her cosmetics bag was sitting on the vanity. Her robe was draped over the end of the bed, which had been made while we were gone. The curtains over the balcony had been drawn back to display the stunning view. And, most importantly, a tiny coffee table had been placed out there, a private place from which she can sit and enjoy the outdoors as much and as often as she'd like. As thrilled as Karesh said she seemed about just having a window in her other room, I figured a balcony would seal the deal.

And it did.

She turned bright eyes and a quietly beaming smile on me. "Thank you. It's beautiful here."

"It doesn't hold a candle to you."

"I'm so tickled, I'm not even going to comment on the quality of that line," she quipped.

"I'm sure I'll hear about it later."

She laughed. "Probably."

Now, I'm waiting for her to arrive at the big table set on the upper deck. Once she realized we'd be having a gourmet breakfast with my clients, she wanted a few extra minutes to make herself "presentable." So I honored her wishes, as hard as it was to leave her there to get dressed all on her own.

We are just being served coffee, making small talk, when Karesh finds me at the table. "Anything else I can get for you, sir?"

"No. And the arrangements you made for Kennedy were perfect. Thank you."

He nods. "My pleasure, sir. I'm glad it worked out."

Jeremy Hobbs, an early-thirties IT guy who made a killing off some malware he developed, speaks up before Karesh can leave. "I think I'd like the beautiful red-head to join me this morning. Will you send her up?"

Karesh glances quickly at me before nodding. "Of course, sir. I'll let her know."

"Got tired of that one already, did you, Spencer?" asks Nathan Todd, a young philanthropist that has a few...risqué proclivities that he likes to keep on the down low. And I, of course, can make that happen.

"Amber's a beautiful woman," I say, skirting the question. Few clients take the same voyage on the same boat with the same crew, but Nathan is one of those few. He was interested in Amber the last time he was onboard, but *she* was only interested in entertaining me behind closed doors. And that's always a choice I leave to each crew member. They're all tested, as are my clients, in case they decide to take matters further, but what happens during the cruise is always consensual, never expected.

"Holy god, who ordered *her?*" Nathan says, completely ignoring me as he looks over my shoulder. I turn to see Kennedy walking toward us. She has this sexy, slinky walk that I doubt she's even aware of, but it's hot as hell. Still not as hot as her, though. If her walk is attractive, then she herself is jaw-dropping.

Her eyes are practically glowing between her dark lashes and her lips are stained just the right amount of pink. They look like ripe peaches, begging to be tasted. Her hair is piled on top of her head with a few pieces hanging loose, curled and left to dangle to her bare shoulders. She's wearing a straight, white dress with straps that cross over the tops of her breasts and tie behind her neck. A gold hoop in the center of her sternum gives a teasing glimpse of her cleavage and I'd bet my left nut that she's not wearing a bra.

I hear the scuff of chair legs and I look around to find every man at the table rising when she stops in front of me. She looks around at each of them, nodding and smiling in a blanket gesture before turning those translucent eyes on me.

"Good morning," she says as though we haven't spent most of it together already.

"Why don't you come sit by me, princess?" Eldon Crisp asks.

"Why would she want to sit with you, old man?" Nathan asks. "She needs something a little more exciting."

"She'd be out of luck with you then," Jeremy says acerbically before turning to address Kennedy directly, "Sweetheart, I promise I could make this the best month of your life."

"What the hell, Hobbs? You just asked to have someone brought up!" Eldon gripes.

"I'd gladly trade for this one."

I clear my throat, suppressing the sudden urge to thump my chest and then beat the shit out of everyone at the table. I have to remind myself that this is, after all, what they're here for. Only not with Kennedy, but they don't know that. "Gentlemen, this is Kennedy and she's joining me for breakfast this morning. And every other morning," I add sharply, meaningfully.

I can only hope that they get the message loud and clear because something tells me I could very easily get violent over Kennedy. Normally, my clients can have anyone they're interested in as long as that person is interested as well. I've never made someone off limits. Never cared enough to. But this time is different. This *person* is different. I'd gladly offend one or two or *all of them* if they so much as breathe in her direction. Offend or tear limb from limb, either way.

Silence falls across the table as I scoot out the empty chair beside me for Kennedy. She smiles up into my face as she gracefully takes her seat. She sits primly on its edge as coffee is poured for her and the first course of fresh tropical fruit is served. As the morning wears on, she eats and chit-chats with my clients as though she has lived her life on a yacht surrounded by the wealthy, rather than roughing it as the hired help on one.

As the dishes are being cleared for the main course to be served, Amber arrives, looking very...voluptuous in a tight, black sheath that hugs every curve and valley. She gives me a brilliant smile, but it falters when she sees Kennedy beside me.

I'm all too familiar with feminine cat fights and how vicious the fairer sex can be toward one another. It's for that reason that my protective instincts surface and I give Amber a warning look as she takes her seat beside the waiting Jeremy.

Much to my relief, she doesn't bare her claws and the men seem to behave themselves. No asses will have to be kicked. Of course, the day is young.

When breakfast is over, everyone disperses, either returning to their room or heading to the gym to work out as we all await the readying of the upper deck. The ship's male staff shuffles out to begin breaking down the table and removing the chairs from the raised dais on which we sat for our morning meal. After that, they'll dismantle the platform in order to reveal the pool underneath, which will be enjoyed by all throughout the rest of the day.

As they work, I lead Kennedy to the railing along the bow of the ship, the place where I saw her standing the night we left Marina del Ray. I tuck her between me and the railing, pressing my chest into hers, loving the way she fits me so perfectly, the way she sort of melts into me. I'm not even sure she's aware of it, but I sure as hell am.

"Mr. Spencer, please!" she exclaims softly with mock outrage. "I'm your employee!" She glances over my shoulder to make sure no one can see us. I don't know who's back there, nor do I care. My attention is focused squarely on the gorgeous female turning to butter against me.

"Fine, you can have the rest of the day off then," I say as I dip my head to rub my lips over hers.

"I didn't work yesterday. Or the day before that. Or—."

I silence her arguments by flicking my tongue over the silky inside of her lower lip, my mouth watering at the sweet taste of her.

"I didn't say anything about this evening. You're getting paid to dance, so you'll dance."

She leans back to look at me, her eyes a mixture of things I couldn't begin to fathom. "I'm dancing?"

"You're dancing. But until then, you're mine," I tell her, spinning her in my arms to press her front into the V of the railing. "All mine."

I run my hand around her waist and up between her heavy breasts to her throat, urging her head back toward me. I lick her from her collarbone to the shell of her ear as I rub my cock against the top curve of her ass.

"Wear something just for me today. Something you know I'll love. Will you do that for me?" I ask.

I can hear her accelerated breathing as I drag my hand back down the valley of her cleavage, my wrist skimming over the hard peak of one nipple. "Yes," comes her breathy reply.

"Just for me," I repeat.

"Just for you."

Reluctantly, I release her, backing away. "Why don't you get changed while I talk to Karesh about arrangements for tonight?"

Kennedy turns to face me, her cheeks flushed, her eyelids at half-mast. "You're evil. You know that, right?"

I wink at her. "Oh, you have no idea."

It's harder than I ever thought it would be to turn and walk away.

CHAPTER TWENTY-EIGHT

KENNEDY

As I sift through all the beautiful clothes that are now tucked safely into the drawers and hanging in the closet of my new room, I rack my brain for something that Reese might like.

"I can't very well go up there naked," I say to the empty room, giggling at the thought of what his reaction might be. My laughter dies when I think of all the other eyes that would see, though. An exhibitionist, I'm not.

I'm still struggling to come up with just the right thing to wear when I come across a plain gray sweatshirt. It reminds me of something Reese told me years and years ago. If he sees me in this, he'll remember that he told me and know that I had him in mind when I dressed. But it's not appropriate for a day by the pool. No, it'll have to wait for tonight. And so will Reese.

With an excited smile in place, I pick out a suit and cover-up combo that shows off my curves in just the right way and complements my coloring. Although it won't be as much for Reese as tonight's outfit will be, knowing that he'll be thinking of taking it off me makes me certain he'll love it just the same.

I slide my feet into a pair of strappy gold sandals and grab some sunglasses and sunblock before perching on the edge of the bed to call Karesh. Reese isn't the only one who needs help with arrangements sometimes.

Twenty-five minutes later, I'm making my way across the polished wood of the upper deck toward what looks like a party that's erupted in the short time I was gone. Three of the four men that I met at breakfast are scattered around the pool area and two men that I've never seen before are in the hot tub with two girls that I've not yet met. Jeremy, the last of the four men that attended breakfast, is rubbing oil on a scantily-clad Amber up on the small sun deck to the left of the bar.

Music is playing in the background and talking, laughing and splashing can be heard from nearly every direction. I can finally see what it is that these men pay for. It's like living a dream for a few weeks—an endless parade of bright sun, vast sea, bottomless drinks, and beautiful women. The fun never ends and I have no doubt that there is much more entertainment aboard than just dancing. Here, there is the distinct possibility of getting laid in a judgment-free, disease-free, consequence-free environment.

I don't even realize I've stopped at the edge of the shade to stare at the scene until Reese appears at my right. "Is something the matter?"

For some reason I feel like crying. It's ridiculous, I know, but the urge is there nonetheless.

"So this is what they pay for. This is how you make your money. Providing a few weeks of hedonism to a bunch of bored, horny men with too much money and too much time."

"I sell the fantasy, Kennedy. It's just like in my clubs, only to the next level. These men are here to enjoy great views and great food while they watch beautiful women dance for them, have beautiful women flirt with them. They're basically here to feel better about themselves. They pay me to make their fantasy a reality, to some degree. They eat, they drink, they get to be the men they are in their own heads and then they go back to their boring lives. End of story. Don't confuse this for something it's not."

"It just seems so…sordid."

"It's not. It's exactly what it looks like. It's men paying for the attention of beautiful women."

"But some of them end up having sex."

"Yes some of them will get a little more than just flirtation, but that's up to them."

"It's like a high-end escort service."

"You make it sound like I'm a pimp."

"Are you?" I ask, meeting his eyes directly.

"No, Kennedy. I'm not. I make money paying beautiful women to do very little. Much less than what they'd have to do at any other job in the world. For the most part, all they have to do is show up and smile. Some dance, some sing, some give massages, some serve meals in extravagant dresses. It's just another job. Just like the one you took. I hired you to dance and serve my clients and that's what you've done."

"I have yet to serve one client," I reply dubiously.

Reese grins. "That's because I don't want to have to decapitate someone this early into the trip."

I try to smile, but my mind is still racing back to the scene before me. And Reese's role in it.

"Do you...have you...*been with*...most of these girls?" I can't even look him in the eye as I ask the question, but I have to ask it.

"Does it matter? You've seen my labs."

I turn my astonished eyes up to his. "Of course it matters!"

"Well, it shouldn't. You're the only one I'm interested in spending time with. *Any kind* of time with."

I never even thought to ask if this whole little...*thing* would be monogamous. I just assumed.

"Come on," Reese says, sliding his fingers down my arm to intertwine them with mine. "Let me buy you a drink."

"It's not even lunch time."

"Around here, time means very little. You do what you feel like doing, *when* you feel like doing it."

"What if I feel like going back to my room?"

"Then you should expect some company."

He tugs on my hand again. "Come on. Let me show you how ridiculous this all is."

Reluctantly, I let him lead me out into the sunshine. "Oh, I get the ridiculous part just fine," I mutter dryly.

I hear Reese laugh before he bends to whisper in my ear, "Shhh, don't tell them. They have no idea." He stops about halfway to the pool and turns me toward him. His eyes rake me from head to toe and a slow, sexy smile creeps across his face. "By the way, I love the outfit."

"Oh, this old thing?" I say, fluttering my eyelashes in mock coyness. "I did the best I could for today, but I couldn't find much. But tonight...tonight I'm wearing something just for you. I think you'll really enjoy it."

Reese raises one brow. "Reeeally?"

The look he gives me threatens to make me blush. He's all but licking his lips like a hungry wolf and I'm all but dying to be his next meal.

****

A couple of hours later, as I'm relaxing in the shade, I realize that Reese was right. This isn't as bad as I thought it might be. As I've watched, a couple of the guys seem like they're just really shy. I can see where that could be a problem for them in real life. But not here.

Most of the others seem well-adjusted, if a little playboy-ish. I think they're here for the fantasy, like Reese says. But there's one or two, particularly Nathan and Jeremy, that give me an uneasy feeling. Something about each of them reminds me of watching a predator. And not in a good way. Even though I have nothing to base it on, I get the feeling that they could get a little rough and insistent. Maybe *too* insistent. It makes me glad that Reese has more or less staked his claim on me. I'd hate to find myself alone with either one of the two. I'm not sure I'd know what to do. At *Exotique*, we didn't have to worry about things like this. There was ample security and the creepers were usually weeded out pretty quickly.

My eyes find Reese. He's embroiled in a conversation about stocks and looking in no hurry to move, so when the breeze picks up and gives me a chill, I decide to head for one of the two raised decks to warm myself in the sun. I choose the one to the right of the bar. The one that Amber is *not* occupying.

My eyes are closed and my face is tilted to the sun when a shadow falls over me. I smile as I crack my lids. I expect to see Reese hovering above me, but instead, I find Nathan.

"Be careful and don't burn. It would be a shame to damage one inch of this beautiful skin." He bends to drag one finger down my thigh as he sits on the end of my lounge chair.

I scoot up into a sitting position, giving him what I hope is a frosty smile. "Thank you for your concern, but I'll be fine. I'm careful. Very careful," I say, emphasizing my last words in case my uninterested smile didn't give him the message.

"Reese always keeps the good ones to himself. Why is that?"

I don't know how to answer that. The only thing I can think of is that I might die if he touches me again. There's nothing overtly bothersome about him. I mean he's not ugly with his dark-blond hair and almond-shaped, green eyes, but there *is* something about him that makes my skin crawl.

Everything that happens next happens so fast, I struggle to take it all in. Nathan is there, sitting next to me one minute and the next minute he's gone. In one quick jerk, Reese grabs him by the back of his shirt, hauls him up and flings him away, sending him careening into two empty chairs as he tries to right himself.

Nathan's expression is comical as his arms flail and he sputters, "What the hell, man?"

Reese's face is positively thunderous. His lips are thin and tight, his fingers are curled into big fists and every muscle in his tall, lean body is stiff as a board. "I told you she's *my* guest."

"I thought it was the girl's choice. Isn't that what you've always said? Isn't that your '*policy*'?" he asks snidely, making air quotes.

"It is my *policy*, except with her. She's mine. You don't touch her, you don't speak to her. You don't even *look* at her. You stay the hell away or I'll throw your ass into the middle of the pacific and you can swim to Fiji."

Nathan's face blazes bright red as he straightens his shirt and tries to regain some of his scattered composure. "That's all you had to say, Spencer. Jesus."

Casting a nasty look over his shoulder, first at Reese then at me, Nathan makes his way off the sundeck and then off the upper deck entirely. I assume he's on his way to his room where he can lick his wounds in private.

Reese looks around at all the eyes fastened on him before he reaches for my hand. Without hesitation, I slip my fingers into his and he pulls me to my feet. His eyes are nearly black with anger and desire and something primitively possessive as he looks down at me.

"Did I mention that you're off the clock today?" he asks.

"Yes," I breathe cautiously.

"Good." With that, he bends his head and gives me a kiss that curls my toes and sears me all the way to my soul. When he's done, he lifts his head, winks at me, brushes his lips over mine again and then turns to our cluster of onlookers. "Any questions?" he asks loudly.

Heads shake all over the deck. Some of the men raise their hands in the universal hands-off gesture. Others simply look away like they don't want to rouse his ire again.

I know I should be insulted. I've just been publicly claimed. But I'm not. It's obvious that Reese has never claimed another girl, at least not like this, and it gives me hope that maybe, just maybe, he really *does* have feelings for me.

"Come on," Reese says, taking my hand. "I'll get Arnold, the captain, to stop us for a couple of hours so we can ride the jet skis."

And, just like that, it's over. He's back to Reese. Calm Reese. Charming Reese. Like nothing ever happened.

The rest of the day goes by in a blur, in a dream-like state of pure happiness. Reese takes me jet skiing out in the pacific. He teases and flirts with me, stopping regularly to pull my vehicle in close enough to his that he can kiss me. And not just light pecks, but *real* kisses, kisses that leave me breathless and wanting.

When dinner rolls around, he's even his charming self around his clients, the clients whom he has blatantly ignored for the majority of the day. It puts me at ease, but I can tell that Nathan is still sore. I can see it in the dirty looks he keeps giving Reese when Reese isn't paying attention. Otherwise, he seems to have moved on. He requested the company of a beautiful platinum-haired server to whom I have yet to be formally introduced. He turns on the charm for her, just as the rest of the men turn on the charm for their chosen company, leaving me to revel in the way that Reese seems to need to touch me all the time.

Every few minutes, whether he's talking to someone else or drinking his wine and listening, he will brush my hand or touch my hair or bump my leg with his under the table. And every time I look at him, no matter what he's doing, he'll glance in my direction. Sometimes he winks, sometimes he smiles and sometimes he just watches me in a way that makes my heart soften like cream cheese on a hot stove.

All in all, it's been one of the best days I've had in a long time, despite the questionable run-in with Nathan. Our easy rapport has made me anticipate my dance tonight even more. I hope he's pleased that I remember something so small from so long ago.

When he drops me off at my room to get ready, he wraps his long fingers around my neck, pushing my hair back over my shoulders before he bends to kiss my pulse. When I feel his tongue sneak out to flicker over it, my arms break out in chills.

"I want you so much I can barely think straight," he moans against my skin. "Remember that when you dance tonight. Remember that you're dancing for me. And no one else."

"Yes," I manage to croak, digging my fingers into his thick biceps to keep from dragging him into my room. "And *you* remember that this dance is specifically for you. Just...remember."

Reese lifts his head, a question burning in his eyes. I smile pluckily, reach around to swat him on the butt and then turn to go into my room. It isn't until my door is closed and I'm leaning against it that I hear his long exhalation. I grin with the knowledge that he's suffering every bit as much as I am. But maybe not much longer. Maybe.

CHAPTER TWENTY-NINE

REESE

I have to make myself sit through the first hour of carefully orchestrated performances. I'm not interested in seeing, hearing or participating in anything that doesn't involve Kennedy.

It's my own fault that she goes on last. Part of that is because I had Karesh add her at the last minute. I know she wants to feel like an employee and I know she loves to dance. But I hate, and I mean hate with a passion that rivals my passion for her, the thought of anyone else having their eyes on her as she dances. It sets my teeth on edge just thinking of how uncomfortable those four minutes will be. But it's for her. If I can just keep that in mind...

When it's finally time for her spot, I find that I'm both excited and testy as hell. I glance left and right to see who's watching. Everyone is. Of course.

I muffle my growl of displeasure.

The lights go dark and I turn my attention back to the stage. When I hear the first notes of the music, I can't help but smile. She said her choice for tonight would really please me. She's already right.

When I was younger, my brothers and I used to watch some of my dad's old movies when he wasn't home, which was often. It was one of those mischievous little things that bond a bunch of young boys for life.

One of my favorites to watch was a tale about a hard-working girl who was a welder by day and a dancer by night. She always wanted to be a ballerina and she met a guy who made that happen for her. My father used to say she was white trash and that nothing like that would ever happen in real life, but I admired her determination, not to mention her hot body and the way she danced. I'm pretty sure that girl gave me at least a dozen of my earliest hard-ons.

I once told Kennedy about it, during that summer so long ago. She said she'd seen the movie and that she loved to watch the girl dance, too. It makes me wonder how much that show influenced both of our lives. I grew up to own dance clubs. Kennedy grew up to dance in one of them. And now, here we are as the girl who has practically nothing and the rich man who can make her dreams come true. Could it be life imitating art?

If we ever had a song, this might be it. And she's playing it for me.

With the first few beats, Kennedy slips quietly out from behind the curtain. Dramatically, she drags her bare toes with each step she takes, her head cast down as she walks. Her slim legs are bare but for the material bunched around her calves. She's wearing a short, skin-tight black skirt and a gray sweatshirt with the neck cut out. It hangs off one shoulder, revealing one narrow, black bra strap. If the music hadn't told me what she was thinking, the sweatshirt would've.

She makes her way to the center of the stage where she dips and sways and twirls like a graceful ballerina. It's easy to see that her talent runs much further than just sexy dancing, although every move she makes is sexy just because she's Kennedy. I don't think she can help it.

Mesmerized, I watch her dance. As the song plays, her moves become more titillating, her eyes swing my way more often. When she spreads her legs into a deep split, her lips part on what looks like a silent moan, like she's remembering me between them. When she bends backward, perfectly displaying her round tits, she closes her eyes like she's feeling me touch her. Everything she does makes my cock that much harder.

It's when she makes her way to the lone chair that I somehow overlooked that I realize what's coming. The lights dim into one spotlight that's focused on her in a single bright beam.

I watch her hand rise to loosen her hair, letting it tumble free in a thick, shiny wave as she arches her back away from the chair. She raises her hand again, this time reaching above her, toward a cord that I can just now see.

I stand to my feet, knowing what comes next. In slow motion, I see her tug. Water falls from out of nowhere, crashing down over her chest and stomach and splashing onto the floor.

She arches her back further and I can hear her gasp clearly, even over the music. Through the wet material of her gray sweatshirt, I can see her nipples harden. As much as I want to taste them, at the moment, all I can think about is how much I hate that anyone else is seeing this, that anyone else is seeing *her*.

My anger rises fast and hot, boiling over before the song even finishes.

"Out!" I shout, loud enough to be heard over the music. There is a pause, during which I turn to scan the room before I repeat, more harshly, "Everybody *out*."

The room clears within a few seconds, the music of some other song left playing in the background. Kennedy is sitting up in her chair, watching me, water dripping from the ends of her hair. When I make my way up onto the stage, she's not moving, not breathing.

Neither am I.

CHAPTER THIRTY

KENNEDY

I see him leap onto the stage with one graceful jump. I see his eyes roving my body like he's deciding what part to attack first. And I see the patience that he's shown me thus far as it dwindles to nothing. Nothing but hunger. Desire. Passion in its rawest, hottest form.

When he reaches me, I know the instant he sets his hands on me that this is going to be a rocket ride to the moon, fast and furious and mind-blowing. And I'm ready for it.

It's time.

His hands go first to my hair, winding into the wet strands and holding my face still for him. His mouth plunders mine. Our tongues tangle, our lips devour.

I feel his hands skate urgently down my arms to curl in the hem of my shirt. He rips it up over my head and flings it to the side. With a growl, he pulls me to him again, bending his head to suck my lower lip into his mouth.

"Tell me you want this as much as I do," he says, his voice dry and hoarse. "Tell me I can do anything I want to you. Right here. Right now."

His words are a spark to dry grass and my insides go up in flames, like a desert wildfire. Heat licks down my spine and burns in the space between my legs.

"Yes. Yes to everything."

That's all he needed to hear. I unchained him, I freed the animal inside, but this time I'm ready for it.

With a savage rip, Reese tears open the back of my bra and pulls it roughly down my arms to bare my breasts to him. When he bends me back over his arm and clamps his lips down over one nipple, I squeeze my thighs together to keep myself from coming apart on the spot.

I thread my fingers into his hair, fisting them in my own frenetic need. When he straightens me, I immediately reach for the front of his shirt, yanking open the buttons in one try.

Reese's hard chest, with its dusting of dark hair, is gleaming with a fine sheen of sweat that makes my mouth water to taste it. So I do. I lean forward and drag my tongue up the dent between his pecs, detouring to take one flat, masculine nipple into my mouth.

He cups my head and hisses when I bite down. "Damn you," he spits in what almost seems like anger.

"I didn't want it to be this way, but you're driving me crazy."

My eyes lock on his as I shake free of his grasp. In this moment, I realize that I *want* to drive him crazy. I *want* him to feel as desperate, as wanton as I feel.

Dropping to my knees in front of him. My fingers work nimbly at the button and zipper of his pants. I part them, pushing them half way down his thighs.

He's not wearing any underwear and my breath sticks in my throat when I come face to face with his enormous cock. I'd forgotten how big it is. That hasn't changed. But one thing has. There, going through the smooth, round head of his penis, is a gold-stud barbell.

I'm fascinated as I look at it. I raise my hand to stroke it with one fingertip. He jerks in response.

"Do you like that?" he asks softly. "It's called a Prince Albert piercing." He exhales, the end of his breath rising in a hiss. "I can't wait to show you what it feels like when I rub you from the inside with it. I want you screaming my name when you come." Reese's voice is like rough velvet rasping along my skin, touching me in all the right places.

I lean forward to swirl my tongue around the studs. His answering groan and the way his fingers curl into my hair send moisture pouring into my panties.

When I close my lips around the head, Reese twitches, reaching to pull me to my feet and up into his arms. His lips crush mine in a kiss that I fear might set me on fire if it weren't for the puddle of water I'm standing in.

Reese kicks off his pants the rest of the way and swings my legs off the floor to lay me down on the wet stage. The cool water at my back has my nipples puckering into painfully tight nubs, which Reese attacks with his lips and his tongue and his teeth. He lifts his chest off me and I feel his hands pulling at my skirt, shoving it and my panties down my legs. He even drags the warmers from my calves.

As soon as I'm practically bare beneath him, his mouth is on the move. He kisses and caresses a hot path down my stomach to the triangle between my legs. My whole world seems centered on that one spot and how much I need to feel his touch there. He nuzzles me with his face, but the touch is light and brief, giving me no relief.

Just before I give in and beg him to put an end to my misery, Reese rolls me onto my stomach. The cold water hits every surface of my front and makes me gasp. The skin of my backside is still cool from lying on the wet stage, making the first touch of Reese's hot mouth almost painful. His tongue at the base of my spine sends shivers through me and the feel of his scorching palms on the curves of my hips steals my breath.

Reese spreads his fingers around my hipbones, tugging them up off the floor, arching my lower body toward him. He drags his lips alongside the crease of my butt before nudging my legs apart. There is a pause where my heart completely stops inside my chest before I feel his lips at my entrance.

I'm helpless against the onslaught of his torture. Reese holds me spread before him, his lips and tongue working white-hot magic between my folds and over my clit as his thumb delves just into my entrance, only to back out again. All I can do is lie prone beneath him, rocking against his mouth as he brings me to the edge.

Just as my orgasm breaks, as though he could taste it hit, Reese rolls me over onto my back, throws my legs over his shoulders and buries his face against me, licking and sucking and fingering me through the waves of my release.

Before my body can completely recover, Reese rises and sits back on his haunches then slides between my legs. I look up at him, his eyes like aqua coals burning from the center of his ravenous face, and I know there is more to come. Much more.

"That piercing that you were so interested in," he begins gruffly, "I want you to feel it rub you on the inside you while you look into my face. I want to see the flash of gold slide in and out of you. I want to see your come dripping off of it."

I feel my muscles contract at his words, grasping at him where he sits at my entrance. My mind is fuzzy with passion, but one thing shines through, like the bright light of panic breaking through early-morning fog.

"I don't have a condom," I admit breathlessly.

"You don't need one. I've had a vasectomy."

I know I'll feel differently about that later, but right now, I only feel relief. And a surge of desire at his next words. "God, how glad I am for that. I want to feel every inch of you, every drop. And I want you to feel every inch of me, stretching you tight, shooting come deep inside you."

"Oh, god," I moan, tightening my legs around Reese.

I watch him as he reaches down and spreads my folds, his fingers massaging my clit as he teases my entrance with his thick head. I glance down and see the light glinting off the golden stud and I feel more heat gush into my core.

"Now, Reese," I plead.

"I need to go slow. I don't want to hurt you," he says, his voice strained as he guides his tip into me, still toying with my most sensitive part.

My mouth falls open as I watch the gold stud disappear into me. He eases it ever so slightly in and out in short, choppy strokes. I can feel the gold balls moving against me, the kind of friction that makes my belly tighten and brings me one step closer to absolute annihilation. I rock my hips toward Reese, trying to take in more of him, but I meet resistance. He's just so big.

"Easy. After you adjust to me, I'll give you what you want. I'll give it to you until you beg me to stop."

I'm panting. I'm dizzy with what he's doing to me, with the bright spotlight shining into my eyes, with the voracious look on Reese's face.

I lift myself up onto my elbows, certain that I can't take one more second. Reese grunts and I see his jaw clench. "Kennedy," he warns, stilling himself with just a couple of inches inside me.

"Reese, I can't wait. Please."

I know I look desperate. I know I sound desperate. I can hear it in my voice, the needs of my body leeching out into my tone. But I feel like the world might explode around me if Reese doesn't fill me. Completely fill me.

I can hear his heavy breathing. I can see the sheen of perspiration on his forehead where he's holding back. His eyes search mine. "Are you sure?"

"I'm sure," I reply without hesitation.

After only a short pause, Reese leans forward, pulls my left leg over his shoulder and thrusts hard into me. For a moment, I feel faint the pleasure is so intense. His overwhelming presence inside me is pure ecstasy and with the friction of the studs as he pulls out and thrusts back in, even deeper if that's possible, I tumble right back over the edge.

My gasp melts into a strangled moan and Reese pumps his hips, surging into me as my body clenches around him. "That's it, baby. Come *hard.*" He's unrelenting as he drives me through my second orgasm.

It's as I lie limply beneath him that I feel him pull out in one slow stroke and I look down at him. Reese is rubbing the tip of his finger over the studs. His cock is glistening with my want and, now, so is his finger.

His eyes flick up to mine. In them is passion like I've never seen before. Reese slips the tip of his wet finger into his mouth, his eyes drifting shut on a groan of pure pleasure. "God, that's the best thing I've ever put in my mouth."

Despite my spent body, a spark flares between my legs as I watch him spread my folds and ease back into me. "Now let me fill you up," he says before he begins his sweet torment all over again. True to his word, Reese fills me up when he reaches his own climax. He doesn't stop until I can feel it running down onto the floor beneath me.

In the end, it's my third orgasm that does me in. I'm so overcome with intense pleasure that I don't even realize I'm screaming Reese's name until I see his smile.

I did it. Just like he said I would.

I was happy to prove him right.

CHAPTER THIRTY-ONE

REESE

Kennedy doesn't object when I dress her, pick her up in my arms and carry her back to her room.

She also doesn't object when I turn on the shower and take her with me into it, fully clothed, only to repeat my invasion of her body all over again. It's when we are lying naked in her bed, curled up beneath the warm covers, her body tucked into the curve of mine, that I begin to wonder why it is that I just can't seem to get enough of her.

"What are you thinking about?" she asks softly from beside me. I had thought she was asleep.

Before I can think better of it, I tell her the truth. "Why it is that I can't seem to get enough of you."

I can almost hear her smile. "Is that a bad thing?"

I pull her in closer to me and kiss the silky skin behind her ear. "Hell no."

"Then why so puzzled?"

"I don't know. I just...I just feel like I don't even know who I am anymore."

I feel her stiffen slightly before she rolls onto her back and turns her head so she can look at me. "You mean because you're with me?"

The sadness and disappointment in her eyes gives me a painful stab in my chest. "God, no! Why would you even think that?"

She shrugs casually, but I know she feels anything but nonchalant. "It's not like I'm exactly 'acceptable' in your world."

"Who gives a shit? I've spent my whole life trying to be someone I'm not. Now, all these years later, I'm just...angry."

Kennedy reaches up and strokes my cheek, her eyes big, green pools of something sweet and safe and real. "You don't have to be anybody but Reese with me."

"But do you even know who I am?"

My question surprises her. She has no answer.

"Do you really want me to be the guy who could just leave you like I did? Because I don't think I like him very much."

"We all grow and change with time, Reese. You don't have to be exactly like that guy anymore. You can be anyone you want to be."

"One thing hasn't changed in all these years."

"What's that?" she asks, her fingertips making lazy circles over my jawbone.

"I don't think I've ever stopped feeling what that nineteen year old boy felt. Since the day I left you, all I can ever remember being is angry. Everything else was just a...a...façade. A mask. A pose for someone else's benefit. To convince people that I'm something I'm not."

"You mean your father?"

I nod. "And others. I've built an empire by showing people that I'm a shrewd, ruthless businessman who can't be taken advantage of. Just like my father. Yet I've spent a lifetime trying to be anything *but* him. As it turns out, I've been walking in his footsteps all along."

"It's not too late to start over, Reese. It's never too late."

I stare into Kennedy's eyes, into her beautiful face. "I wish it was that easy."

"It can be."

I smile and kiss her on the end of her nose, but I make no comment. She probably wouldn't say that if she knew everything about me.

No, she wouldn't say that at all.

CHAPTER THIRTY-TWO

KENNEDY

I've never felt more like a princess than I do when I'm with Reese. Well, I've actually never felt like a princess *at all* until Reese. He had this way of making me feel special when we were younger. That's something that hasn't changed. He makes me feel like I'm the only girl in the world.

He's hardly left my side for a minute since the night he found me in my room, sea sick. During the day, he'll go for a few minutes here and there to take care of business with Karesh or make a few necessary phone calls, but it's usually when I'm changing clothes for dinner. Otherwise, every morning he's curled around me when I wake up, he's putting his hands all over me in the gym as he works me out, he's giving me the royal treatment as we lie by the pool and then he's hiding away with me at night, making love to me in breathtaking ways. It's been the most surreal experience of my life.

He hasn't asked me to dance again either. He did manage to apologize the morning after my last dance, though. The morning after that crazy encounter on the stage.

I woke to the fine tickle of something along my side. I reached around to brush it away, only to find it was Reese's hand.

"Your skin is like the finest silk in the world," he'd purred by my ear. At that point, he'd abandoned the light tickling and started to stroke his palm up and down my side. "I'm sorry if I embarrassed you last night."

"How did you embarrass me?" I asked, starting to squirm as his hand moved further and further toward my front, skimming the edge of my breast all the way down to the inside of my hipbone and back again.

"By clearing the room," he said, dragging his palm up between my breasts and then back down again. His fingertips stopped just at the apex of my thighs, causing a thrill to precede them and land in my core like a bolt of lightning. On his next trip up and down, I found myself anticipating his arrival there, hoping he'd touch me like I wanted him to.

"Yes, how horrible of you to do what you want to do on your own ship. It was scandalous," I teased, trying to be patient and wait for him to make the first move.

When his hand found its way to the bottom of my stomach again, I eased my legs open the tiniest bit in invitation, but still he stopped just short of the throb there.

"You don't know how conflicted I was. This is my boat and these are my clients and that's the kind of entertainment I promise them. But not you. Never you. I loved seeing you up there, but knowing that they were watching you..." He trailed off, his touch growing rougher, more insistent as he trekked back up my stomach to cup my breast. "Knowing that they were watching your nipples get hard under that water..." He pinched my nipple then, tugging it as though the memory still aggravated him. I sucked in a breath and I waited, fighting the urge to arch my back and press my butt into his groin. "Knowing that they were wishing they could put their hands on you," he said, moving down to the ache that seems only to burn for him, "to put their fingers inside you. Their cocks."

Suddenly, as though he was urgent to lay claim to me once more, Reese reached down and pulled my top leg over onto his, spreading my thighs wide for him. He dipped one finger inside me, thrusting hard and deep. His groan must've been from finding me soaking wet for him, for then he shifted behind me and entered me in one quick, sharp motion.

We both gasped and then exhaled at the same time, neither having grown accustomed to that incredible feeling. Conversation stopped at that point. Reese parted my folds with his fingers and rubbed my clit until I could do nothing but say his name over and over and over again.

He came with me that time. I felt him stiffen behind me just as he poured heat deep into me, thrusting again and again until I lay boneless in his arms.

Afterward, he pulled out of me but he left my leg on top of his. As he kissed my shoulder and nuzzled my neck, he fingered me ever so gently, whispering wonderful things into my ear.

"I love the way you feel inside, so smooth, so wet with my come," he said, stroking my walls with his finger. "I wish I could stay in you forever."

I thought to myself that I wish he could, too.

Every morning since then has been spectacular like that. And every night has been even better.

Today marks our first port since Hawaii—the Marquesas Islands, which I know nothing about. It's also the first morning I've awakened to an empty bed. But it's not long until I hear the creak of the cabin door and I see Reese sneaking back in.

I feign sleep to see what he's going to do. He has the most delicious ways of waking me up and I'd hate to miss one because I woke too early.

I feel his weight as he crawls across the bed toward me, my insides curling with anticipation. He first nuzzles my neck before he sucks the lobe of my ear into his mouth. "Rise and shine, beautiful," he whispers, his hand rubbing gentle circles over my butt.

I stretch and give him a sleepy smile, pretending to wake. His eyes are bright and twinkling with excitement.

I tilt my head to get a better look at him. "You look awfully chipper this morning."

"I'm anxious to get ashore, that's all," he says, giving me just enough of a kiss to make me want more.

Reese hops over me to land on the floor beside the bed then reaches for my hands and drags me into a sitting position. The sheet falls away from my naked torso, drawing his eye. His pupils dilate, his eyes taking on that dark, hungry look that I'm becoming so familiar with.

I don't bother to cover myself, mainly because I'm already missing our morning romp. With his appreciative gaze settled on my chest, my nipples pucker prettily as if trying their best to lure him back to bed.

"Damn," he says on a sigh, shaking his head. "You should probably be illegal in at least thirty countries. You're addictive."

I laugh. "Wanna come get your fix then?" I ask, leaning back on my elbows, an obvious invitation.

Reese doesn't give me his usual cute comeback. He doesn't jump my bones either. Instead, he walks slowly toward the bed and takes one strand of hair that's lying over my heart. His eyes never leaving mine, he says, "One more fix will never be enough, I'm afraid." His voice is quiet, sincere. A bit cryptic even.

He raises his hand to cup the side of my face. He stares at me for several long, intense seconds before his expression clears and he says with more of his earlier enthusiasm, "Put on your suit and some shorts. I'm taking you out."

I smile and climb out of bed. "Okay," I tell him, doing my best to hide both my disappointment and my worry over his statement. While that *should be* a good thing, Reese didn't seem too thrilled with becoming addicted to me. I don't know what to think about his reaction. So I'll ignore it. Like I've been ignoring all unpleasant things of late. They'll come back around soon enough and I'll deal with them then.

Less than an hour later, Reese and I are hiking up the Marquises Rando on Nuku Hiva. Having been here numerous times, Reese tells me stories of local legend and tales of people he's encountered on previous trips. He helps me up steep spots and holds my hand when we stop to enjoy the view.

At the top, as though by magic, awaits Sven, one of the male waiters that I met a couple of days ago. He's holding a big basket over a pristine white blanket that's spread out on the grass.

"Breakfast is served, m'lady," Reese says, bowing formally and sweeping his arm toward the blanket.

I don't even know what to say as I kneel on the soft material and Reese comes to lounge beside me. We are quiet as Sven unpacks a breakfast of gourmet egg-and-sausage burritos, fresh fruit, orange juice and sparkling water.

As we dig in, I don't even notice Sven leaving. I only know that nearly an hour later, I look up and he's nowhere to be found.

"He'll be back to take all this to the yacht," Reese explains like he read my mind.

"Do you treat all your...women this way?" I sip my orange juice as I consider him. He looks like Adonis bathed in tropical sunlight, more magnificent than any of the views I've seen.

"You're not one of my 'women'," he says lightly, tilting his head to the side as he considers me right back. "And I don't want you thinking you are."

I don't know what to say to that, so I say nothing.

"I want to show you everything. I want to buy you everything. I want you to have the kind of pleasures that someone like you deserves."

"I appreciate that, Reese, but I don't deserve any of this."

He shrugs. "I think you do. I want you to have the best of everything."

"But I don't need it. I'm not that kind of a girl."

"But you could be."

"No, I'll never be like that. This is who I am, Reese. Simple. Plain. Average."

"There's nothing simple or plain or average about you. I don't know why you can't see that."

It's my turn to shrug. "Because it's just the way it is."

"Well then maybe I can change all that," he says, leaning over to peck my cheek before he rises to his feet and reaches for my hand. "Come on. We've got lots to see today."

I assume that Sven cleans up our mess after we leave to head back down to sea level. Once there,

Reese takes me back to the shore where a smaller boat is waiting.

We speed across a short stretch of ocean to a place Reese tells me is Hiva Oa. We tie the boat at a small dock there and he takes me to see the resting place of Gauguin, as well as a local museum dedicated to his art. We walk hand in hand along the street, talking like we've known each other all these years rather than like we've been separated all this time. It's bittersweet because I know it will end at some point and we'll soon be strangers again.

After an afternoon snack that was stashed in the cool storage of the boat, we head back out to sea to make another fairly short trip to Fatu Hiva, where we enter through what's called the Bay of Virgins.

Reese guides the boat in between huge rock formations that rise up out of the water on three sides. The sun is shining brightly on the peaks and dappling the water with rays of gold. Reese stops the boat and drops anchor about twenty yards from where the rocks converge and there's nothing around us but steep cliffs and a trickling waterfall.

"Care for an afternoon swim?" he asks, kicking off his shoes.

He doesn't have to ask twice. It's hot here and the water looks cool and refreshing. Reese strips down to his shorts and dives in, surfacing just in time to watch me dive in beside him. Together we swim to the apex of the rock formation. It's there, without a single word said, that Reese pulls me into his arms, stares deeply into my eyes and makes love to me in the warm French Polynesian waters.

It's like that at every group of islands we visit. He takes me to a handful of amazing locations, buys me beautiful things and makes love to me somewhere unusual, like he's marking the spot. Whether that's what he intends, it's certainly what's happening in my mind. And in my heart. I'll never think of this half of the world the same way again, without an ache that will likely never go away.

At some ports, our stay is longer. Reese always has some stunning accommodations lined up. In Bora Bora, we stayed in a little cottage that overlooked the sea. We slept in a bed surrounded by netting and made love all night long while the flicker of the fire just outside the open doors bathed our skin in a warm, orange glow.

In Tahiti, we stayed in a *bure*, a private bungalow that sits at the end of a pier, perched high over the water. Our breakfast was delivered by a man in a canoe. We ate bagels and cream cheese and licked fresh coconut juice from each other until well into the afternoon.

Despite our earlier conversation, Reese still insists on showering me with everything from expensive clothes to sparkling jewelry to thousand-dollar-an-ounce perfume. I want for nothing, but all I really want is Reese.

After Tahiti, we got back on the yacht for a longer trek to Fiji. This morning Reese told me we would be in port later tonight and that he wanted to take me to the show upstairs for a change. It's the last one for a few days since everyone will be on shore enjoying the island. This marks the last stop before the return journey home.

I've been excited all day. For some reason, it feels like a date. Even though we've spent every waking minute together for weeks, he's kept me hidden away from everyone else on board and this feels like some kind of statement. I just don't know what it says.

I'm still in my robe, putting on my makeup when I hear a knock at the door. I go to answer it, expecting to see Reese, but instead I find Karesh.

He does that tiny bow of his head that he always does before he smiles. "Ms. Moore."

As always, I give him the same small bow and smile. "Mr. Karesh." His grin always deepens. I have no idea what his last name is. Or if Karesh *is* his last name. Either way, it's become a bit of a game between us over these weeks.

He hands me a plain white box with a big, gold ribbon wrapped around it and tied in a perfect bow. "A gift from Mr. Spencer. He asks that you wear it tonight. He'll be waiting for you at the bow of the ship, on deck. Seven sharp."

With that, he nods again and then turns to walk away. I lean out into the hall and call after him, "Thank you."

I see his head tip back a bit and hear a faint, "My pleasure." That makes me smile. He might, just *might*, be warming up a little.

I shut the door and scurry to the bed to open the box. Inside it, beneath a mountain of soft, white tissue paper, is a dress. A beautiful dress. One of a zillion nice things he's bought me.

The color reminds me of an emerald—that rich, deep green. The material feels like velvet and it's heavy as I hook my fingers under the straps and pull it out of the box.

The dress falls in a smooth drape all the way to the floor. The waistline is subtle as it runs into the puckers that will gather from beneath my breasts to join at the jeweled medallion in the center. The plunging neckline is asymmetrical and the left strap is much wider than the right, giving the appearance that there is only one. I turn it around and find that the asymmetry is carried to the back. The line falls drastically from ribs-high on the left side to where it rejoins the green velvet at my right hip, leaving the majority of my back exposed.

It's stunning. It's daring. It's elegant. And Reese bought it for me to wear. Tonight.

The tag is still in place, although the actual cost has been torn away. There is simply the name of a boutique, written in fancy script, as well as another name, one I assume belongs to the dress.

I drape it across the bed and take the matching shoes from the bottom of the box. They are open-toed heels covered in jewels that match the centerpiece of the dress. I'm not accustomed to extravagant gifts like this. The best I can hope for is that I will take Reese's breath away when he sees me in it.

When I'm dressed and surveying myself in the mirror, I wonder what Reese will see. Will he see simply the wide sage eyes rimmed with dark lashes and ringed in smoky shadow? Will he see the sun-kissed cheeks and ruby-red lips? Or will he see the sparkle in my eye that says I never stopped loving him? That I'm already deeper in love with him than I ever was as a girl?

I can admit my situation to myself much more easily than what I would've imagined. I think the moment I agreed to give Reese a chance, I knew what would happen. In a way, I had to be okay with it before I ever took the first step. I knew then just like I know now that Reese nearly destroyed me once, and that he might do so again, but I'm helpless to stop it. I'll love him until there's nothing left. And then long after. It's inevitable. *He's* inevitable.

I turn away from my reflection and walk toward the door. There's no place to go but forward. I learned a long time ago that I can never go back.

The wind is calm up on deck. The air is dry and warm, and it's quiet but for the lively conversation drifting through the windows from the dining room. My heels make a soft clack on the deck boards as I head around toward the bow. When I take the final three steps that put me up on the platform, I see Reese leaning against the railing. The sea breeze is ruffling his dark hair and the orange blaze of the setting sun is illuminating half his handsome face, giving his eyes that pale, fathomless sparkle of these tropical waters.

Although he was already motionless, he seems to stop when he sees me, stop breathing even. Much like I have. His eyes roam me from the curls piled intricately atop my head to the red-painted toes peeking out from my dazzling shoes. It gives me time to adjust to seeing him in his finery. He looks more dashing than James Bond in his black suit and crisp white shirt, holding a glass in one hand and a box in the other.

"You take my breath away," he rumbles when I stop a few inches from him.

My smile feels like it might outshine the sun when I admit, "I was hoping I would, but I forgot all about it when I saw you standing here."

Like he doesn't want to break me, Reese straightens and dips his head to brush his lips across mine. Even the light contact incites a zing of excitement, just like it always does. Reese—his presence, his attention, his touch—brings every molecule of my being into pinpoint focus on him. It's like the rest of the world doesn't exist. And I don't want it to.

Reese reaches behind me to set his glass on a small, linen-draped table that I only just now noticed before he straightens and opens the box he's holding.

"For you. Nothing half as beautiful as you are, but I wanted you to have it anyway."

In the long, rectangular box lays a wide bracelet encrusted with the same jewels as my dress and shoes, although I suspect these might be real. Rubies, sapphires, emeralds and a few diamonds chase each other in row after row of glittering gemstones.

Reese takes it out of the box and winds it around my wrist, securing it before he brings my hand to his mouth and kisses my knuckles. "Thank you for coming with me this summer. I didn't realize how much I needed you until you came back into my life."

My heart is slamming against my ribs like head-bangers in a mosh pit. "Thank you for bringing me. I...I..."

Reese's lips curve into that sexy, lopsided smile that I love. "No need to thank me. I assure you, *you* are one hundred percent my pleasure."

Heat flares between us in an instant. It's hard for me to keep my hands off him as he leads me to the table and pulls out my chair for me. I think he's feeling the same way if the ravenous look in his eyes is any indication, but he wants this night for some reason. For me? For us? I don't know, but I'll go along with anything he wants to do. Anything, anytime anywhere.

Sven is our waiter again. He brings us course after course of the most delicious food I've ever tasted. Reese and I enjoy every bite of it, sometimes feeding each other, sometimes laughing about him using his fingers rather than his fork, sometimes just enjoying the amazing view and the even more amazing company. The whole scene is like something from a movie or a fairy tale. I squash down the niggling nugget of dread that has yet to vacate the very pit of my stomach, the one that is braced for the disaster that should come when any situation is this perfect.

After dinner, Reese and I have another glass of wine before he takes me to the showroom and leads me to a small table for two set near the stage. Together we enjoy the entertainment, including two increasingly risqué dances by Amber, followed by a beautiful piano being rolled out onto the stage.

I'm curious as to who plays when I see none other than Brian take a seat behind it. He plays several songs like a classically-trained pianist and it seems everyone appreciates it.

When it's over, the lights come back on and everyone gets up to leave. Reese doesn't move to get up, so I keep my seat until he's ready. He sits in the chair to my left, just watching me, for at least five minutes after the room has completely emptied out. Finally, when the lights dim again, leaving only enough illumination for us to see the piano clearly, Reese stands, offering me his hand. I slide my fingers into his and let him guide me to the three steps that lead onto the stage.

Reese walks to the piano, stops and turns toward me, circling his hands around my waist to lift me onto it. He angles me toward the front as he takes a seat on the bench.

Gracefully, he runs his fingers over the keys, every bit as expertly as Brian had.

"You play?" I ask in surprise.

"I play," he replies with a smile.

After a few bars, the notes begin to take on those of a song I recognize—*Fever*. The sensual tune seeps into the air like a drug and, immediately, I'm under the influence. I feel it in a physical way, like a touch, a touch that sizzles along the surface of my skin. Suddenly, the heat of the light is hotter, the black lacquer of the piano cooler. My skin is ultra-sensitive, and every cell of my being is waiting for Reese to reach for me. My body strains toward him, eager for that moment.

But then he starts to sing.

I've heard the song performed by a man before, but never has it sounded this good, never has it *felt* this good. His deep voice is like smooth, rich chocolate. Deliciously mesmerizing. Decadently tantalizing.

I watch Reese as he plays. And he watches me.

During the second verse, he stops playing, instead using his hands to grasp my hips and drag me closer to him. He takes off my shoes and sets them aside before gently resting my bare feet on the keys, all the while singing in his low voice. He never takes his eyes off mine as he runs his palms up my calves. When he gets to my knees, he presses against the insides of them, urging me to spread my legs. So I do, anticipation humming through my veins.

My breath is coming in shallow pants as Reese raises my dress with his forearms, stroking his fingers up my thighs. With excruciating slowness, he drags my panties off, brushing them across his mouth before he sets them aside.

When my lower body is bared to him, Reese stands. As he draws closer to me, the words of the song trail off until there's nothing but silence and the sound of his breath colliding with mine.

When our lips meet, it turns into a slow tango of our tongues that turns my toes into ten tiny flames and my belly into a melting pot of the most all-consuming desire I've ever known.

Everything happens in slow motion, as though the song still plays in the background. Reese leans away and stares into my eyes for what seems an eternity before he runs his fingers down my throat and over my chest, pressing gently until I'm lying flat on my back on top of the piano.

I feel every warm breath he exhales as he drags his mouth up the inside of my thigh, using his hands to open my legs wider and wider until I feel the cool air hit the moisture there. With the barest shake of his head, Reese nuzzles me with his lips. The scruff of his stubble scrapes me just barely, robbing me of air and causing my muscles to contract in readiness.

But Reese is only ready to play, not to ease the perpetual ache that resides within me, an ache that burns solely for him. With one fingertip, Reese teases my folds, running it up and down, side to side, all the while swirling his tongue over me with the lightest of touches.

He plays until I feel near screaming, until my level of frustration is near unbearable. But then, as if sensing my threshold, Reese's touch becomes more insistent, firmer. He licks with purpose. He probes with intent. It's when he sucks my clit into his mouth and drives his fingers deep inside me that I feel the implosion in my core.

Penetrating me with his fingers, Reese flicks his tongue over me until I feel the gush of heat and wetness pour through me. Then he's cupping my ass. He's holding me to his mouth. He's moving his lips over me like a man starved of this needful nourishment. And when the tide that washes through me settles into a slow lapping, Reese buries his tongue inside me and licks me until there's nothing left.

When he releases me and reaches for my hands to pull me into a sitting position, he slowly sweeps his tongue through the inside of my mouth.

"You taste like every dream I've had since I was nineteen years old," he says huskily. "I've looked for this all over the world and I couldn't find it anywhere but here."

Reese licks at my mouth and bites at my lips as he unzips his pants. When he pulls me into his arms, my legs wrap automatically around his waist. I can feel his erection touching my butt as he moves to sit on the piano bench.

"I want to watch your face as you come in the sunshine," he whispers, teasing me with the head of his shaft. Already, I feel my passion for him returning, I feel the trickle of liquid as my body prepares for what's to come. "I want to wet my cock in you by the moonlight." With every word that comes out of his mouth, my body reacts, clutching desperately at him. "And I want to make love to you at a piano," he says, raising me up to impale me on his long, broad length.

We both grunt at the same time and then Reese pauses, buried to the balls inside me, and we savor the exquisite fullness of the moment, the feeling of him stretching my body to its maximum.

"There will never be anything but this, but us. You're mine, Kennedy Moore. All. Mine."

Like the flip of a switch, Reese becomes urgent, feral. He slams me down on him over and over, pulling my hair, biting my neck. He growls in my ear, telling me again and again that I'm all his, no one else's.

My orgasm has come and gone again, but Reese is still frantic when he stands. With me still wrapped around him, he leans me into the piano, pounding into me as hard as he can.

"Look at me," he finally says, his voice a hoarse croak.

I do as he asks, watching that angrily possessive light flicker in his eyes. He groans one word as he comes inside me, mutters it over and over again as he pumps hot liquid into me. "Mine."

When we've both regained our breath, Reese sets me on my feet in front of him and helps me into my panties, straightening my dress before he stands to sweep me into his arms. He gives me the gentlest kiss before carrying me back to my room. That night, he makes love to me time and time again, like he's trying to memorize me and the way my body feels under his. It's the most perfect night of my life.

Right up until a woman bursts into my room the next morning.

CHAPTER THIRTY-THREE

REESE

"How could you?" Claire Norton rails when she flings open the door. I don't have a lot of patience to deal with her when I'm wide awake, much less first thing in the morning.

"Hello, Claire," I say, rubbing a hand across my face. "You're looking well." And she is. With her rich black hair and equally black eyes, she looks like a million bucks, which is probably what she spent to get that way.

"You need to kick your latest floozy out right this minute. We have to talk," she fumes.

"Claire," I begin, my temper spiked instantly by her derogatory reference to Kennedy. However, my angry retort is squashed by a small voice.

"Reese, who is this?" Kennedy asks. I turn to find her sitting up in the bed, holding the sheet up to cover her all the way to her chin.

Before I can answer or explain it like it needs to be explained, Claire hisses, "I'm his fiancée, sweetie. Or didn't he tell you about me?"

Oh shit.

I release a heavy sigh. This is not how I wanted to tell her.

I see the color drain from Kennedy's face and, with it, any trust I've managed to build over the past weeks.

"It's not what you think," I assure her, reaching for her hand beneath the covers. She pulls away.

"So she's not your fiancée?" she asks. I can hear the hopeful note in her voice and it kills me to have to listen to it die. I know what she'll think.

"It's a long story. Just…just give me a minute and I'll explain."

I fling back the covers and stalk bare-assed to get my pants where they're folded over the vanity chair, jerking them on angrily. Claire's timing could *not* be any worse.

Half dressed, I stomp across the room to grab Claire by the arm and haul her out of Kennedy's room, closing the door behind me. I release her and yank open the door to my room, waiting for her to come inside before I slam it shut.

"I don't appreciate that kind of entrance, Claire."

"Why?" she asks waspishly, her eyes flashing furiously. "Afraid it might ruin your fun?"

I sigh. I don't have time for this. "What do you want?"

"You promised Daddy no more boats until this deal went through. You promised."

She has to be referring to Sempre.

"I didn't have to touch any money promised to your father to purchase it. I agreed to take on an investor. He's in for forty percent," I snap.

I see some of her indignation flee. "Oh. Well, Daddy doesn't know that."

"Then maybe *Daddy* should've asked before sending his daughter halfway across the world."

"I was vacationing in Fiji, thank you. I thought we could spend some time together when you got into port. As a surprise. But it seems like that isn't going to happen."

"Not when you spring it on me like this, it won't."

Like the last five minutes never happened, a smile curves Claire's glossy mouth and her voice turns to a purr rather than a screech. "This morning was just a misunderstanding, obviously. There's no reason we can't still enjoy the rest of our stay." She closes the distance between us, dragging the backs of her fingers down my cheek. "Especially once you wash off the stink of your latest victim."

I grab her wrist in an iron grip and pull it away from me. "She's not my latest anything, Claire. And no, we won't be spending any time together this trip."

Her bottom lip juts out in a pout. "What a shame. Your father *did* warn me that you like to slum it, though."

I grit my teeth, reminding myself that Claire is, in fact, a woman, therefore I can't physically hurt her. No matter how much I'd like to.

"The best thing you could do right now, Claire, is to get the hell off my boat, get the hell off Fiji and give me some time to cool off."

I walk to the door and hold it open for her. She hesitates only for a few seconds before she glides out into the hall in her beauty-pageant gait.

She continues a few steps before stopping right in front of Kennedy's door, saying loudly enough for practically anyone to hear, including Kennedy, "See you in a few weeks, lover." The smile she gives me before she walks away assures me that she did that very much on purpose.

I wait until I hear the click of her heels on the floors of the lounge above before I go back into Kennedy's room. She's still sitting exactly where I left her, still pale as a ghost, still looking like I cut out her heart and threw it into the ocean.

"God, what an awful way to wake up. Can we just go back to sleep and try that again?" I ask, hoping to diffuse the situation rather than trying to explain it when she's upset.

"You're kidding, right?" she asks.

It was worth a try.

"Of course," I tell her, swallowing my sigh as I sit on the end of the bed. Something tells me she won't want me very close until we get this straightened out.

"Who *was that*, Reese?"

"That was Claire Norton. She's the daughter of a business associate of mine and my father's."

"I don't care about any of that. You know what I'm asking. Was she telling the truth? Is she your fiancée?"

Her voice cracks on the last word, as though she almost choked on it as it came out.

"She is, but it's never been anything more than a business transaction, trust me."

"Trust you?" she whispers. And then more loudly. "Trust you?" Her laugh is bitter and I can see tears glistening in her eyes. "How in the world can you even ask that? We've spent nearly every waking moment together for weeks and you've somehow neglected to mention a tiny detail like the fact that you're *engaged*. Of course I can't trust you, Reese." She gets up and paces to the bathroom door, stunning in her nudity. It's hard for me to ignore, but now is not the time to be appreciating her physical attributes.

"If it were important, I would've told you sooner, but it's just...not. In fact, I haven't given Claire a single thought since I saw you dancing that first night in Chicago. That's how *not a big deal* this actually is."

"Reese! How can you say that? You. Are. Engaged." She pauses, the breath *whooshing* out of her as if the notion just struck her all over again, a physical punch. "To be married. How could this not be a big deal?"

"Kennedy," I say gently, getting up to go to her. Carefully, I place my hands on her shoulders. "It is a business arrangement. Nothing else. There is no love between us. She will never interfere with us. In fact, you'll probably never even *see* her again."

"So your plan is to…to…what? Have us both? Marry her and have me on the side?"

"It's not like that, Kennedy. I'll be married to her in name only. It's just business. Nothing more. She will never mean any more than that to me. She will never mean even a tiny bit as much as what you mean to me."

Her mouth is hanging open and she's staring at me incredulously. "And that doesn't sound the least bit scummy to you?"

"Kennedy, what does it matter if a piece of paper ties my family to hers when it's *you* that has my heart?"

"Reese, you can't give someone your heart and then marry someone else. It just doesn't work that way."

"But why not? Why *can't it* work that way?"

A dark cloud rolls over her beautiful features. "It could *never* work that way with me, Reese. Never. I won't share you."

"You won't be sharing me."

"So you've never slept with her?"

"I didn't say that, but I can tell you that I will never be sleeping with her again. You're the only one I want, Kennedy. Can't you see that?"

"How could I? You've never told me that, and now, when you finally do, it's because your fiancée showed up. What do you expect me to think, Reese? How do you expect me to feel?"

"I had hoped you felt the same way about me that I feel about you."

"Obviously that's not the case. I could never...*would never*...marry someone else if my heart wasn't in it."

"It's just business, Kennedy," I repeat in exasperation. "Stuff like this happens all the time."

"Not in my world it doesn't."

"But my world *is* your world now. We can be together. I promise you that Claire won't be a problem."

For the longest time Kennedy says nothing. I watch the anger and indignation leave her face as an incredible sadness sweeps in. It causes my heart to freeze right inside my chest. I know before she opens her mouth that she'll be saying goodbye.

"I told you I'm a simple girl, Reese. I don't need diamonds or expensive perfumes. I don't need to travel all around the world and eat food that costs more than my rent. All I need is someone to trust. If you can't see that Claire is *already* a problem for me, then you're not the man I thought you were."

When she turns to walk away, fading into the bathroom and closing the door behind her, I know our time has come to an end.

I also know that I can't let her go.

CHAPTER THIRTY-FOUR

KENNEDY

An unbearable explosion is happening in my chest. It threatens my wholeness. As soon as the bathroom door is closed, I fold over, wrapping my arms around myself to hold together the jagged pieces of what used to be me.

I stay like that until my legs start to tingle with numbness. When I rise and stumble to the sink, I see the tear-stained face of a fifteen year old girl who made the mistake of trusting the wrong man fourteen years ago, the *same* man. As bad as that hurt, it now seems insignificant in comparison.

A sob strains against my throat. Stubbornly, I refuse to let it loose. Instead, I turn on the shower in hopes of hiding my grief in the steamy mist and then letting the drain carry it away forever.

Over an hour later, when my face is so red from hot water that tear tracks can no longer be seen, I wrap myself in a towel and march bravely into the next room for my clothes. My heart trips over itself at the renewed pain of seeing Reese sitting on the edge of my bed, his hands clasped between his knees, his eyes pleading.

"Kennedy, please," he says. The words are simple, but it's his voice that tells the tale. It sounds like the raw, gaping wound that now occupies the space where my heart used to be.

"There's nothing left to say, Reese. I'm packing my stuff and staying the night in Fiji. I'll get a flight home from there."

He closes his eyes. "Please don't do this. Please don't go."

"We both knew this was only temporary. I hate that it's ending this way, but something would've happened sooner or later."

I hope my words sound more convincing than they feel. In my heart, I had hoped this would never end, that I'd finally get my happily ever after with the man of my dreams. But I found out long ago that there are no heroes, that there's no Superman waiting to rescue me. It's just me and whatever happiness I can manage to dredge up for myself. Nothing more. Nothing less.

"I didn't want it to end, Kennedy. I wanted us to be together. I still do."

"I'm sorry, Reese. I truly am."

I keep my expression as blank as I can as I walk past him to the closet. I tell myself that if I can just hold it together for a few more hours, I can curl up in a ball in the privacy of some tropical hotel room and give in to the urge to mourn the parts of my heart and soul that have just died.

"Kennedy please. Please don't leave me."

I squeeze my eyes shut against the sting of tears and I bite my lip to hold back another gut-wrenching sob that's welled up inside me. I don't trust myself to speak, to answer him in any way, so I don't. I just pull out a blouse and some shorts and drop my towel to slip them on.

When I turn, the stricken look on Reese's face stops me in my tracks.

"I'm in love with you, Kennedy. You're what I've spent the last fourteen years of my life looking for. I just didn't know it. I didn't know that I was the man I've always wanted to be before I left you. And I've been less of a man every day since. Please don't walk away. I've never begged for a single thing in my entire life, but I'm begging you. Please. Please don't go."

I can't hold it in one more second. The sound is torn from me as though something vicious and awful ripped it out. "Get out, Reese. I can't do this again. I can't survive it. Please. Just get out."

My knees quiver slightly before they give out on me, dumping me in the floor. I cover my face and cry mercilessly into my hands.

I feel Reese at my side before I hear him, like an inescapable gravity pulling me toward him. But I resist. I have to. I know that it'll be a miracle if I survive this much again. I can't let him take what's left. I can't.

When his arm comes around me, I jerk violently away. "Don't touch me! Just get out."

The warmth of his presence recedes as he stands and backs away. I hear his pause and I wait. Finally, after forever has passed and taken a few more pieces of me with it, he walks toward the door. I'm sobbing so loudly, I almost miss his soft words.

"I've loved you from the moment I met you. For fourteen years, I've loved you. And I'll love you for a million more."

I hear another pause before the door opens and then closes with a hushed, final click.

That's when the pain *really* starts.

****

As much as I try to do on my own, being in a foreign place with zero preparation and zero information is more than I can deal with right now. Finally, I enlist Brian's help. I call him and, thankfully, he answers right away.

"Well, hello there, Belle. Has the ball stopped long enough for you to remember us little people?" he asks in his teasing, Disney way.

"Can you come to my room?" I ask without preamble.

The line is quiet for a few seconds. His response tells me he knows the situation is dire. "I'll be right there."

Less than two minutes after the click of the line going dead, there's a muted knock at my door. Hesitantly, I open it a crack, looking to confirm that it's Brian and not Reese.

He pushes past me and closes the door behind himself. "Good God, what happened? You look like you've been run over by a garbage truck."

I'm too numb to even appreciate his colorful analogy. "I need some help finding a place to stay on the island until I can get a flight home. I don't know...I don't know anything about Fiji, I have no money and don't know where to find a bank that'll help an American. Do they have taxis here? Do they have ATMs? Do they have places I can stay at the last minute? I mean...I just don't know anything. I'm so unprepared. I..." I trail off, feeling so overwhelmed, I can't even put my thoughts into adequate words.

"Why do you need any of those things? What happened?"

I look Brian directly in the eye for the first time. I didn't want him to see the wreckage, but maybe seeing it will save me from having to explain it. "Things just didn't work out."

His eyebrows fly up. "That boy is off the market for you. What the hell is that matter with you?"

"He's engaged," I answer simply.

Brian's mouth falls into a silent, round O. It's plain to see that he didn't know either.

When he recovers, he takes my hand in his and gives it a squeeze. "Tell me what you need. I'll make it happen."

I give him a watery smile and squeeze his hand back.

CHAPTER THIRTY-FIVE

REESE

"I found her, sir," Karesh says when I answer. Relief washes through me.

"Where is she?"

"She's staying at a small bed and breakfast in the heart of downtown."

"So she didn't use the *bure* either." It's bad enough that Kennedy is leaving me, but the fact that she won't even let me help her is tearing me up inside. I had Karesh make every conceivable arrangement for her, but she hasn't used any of them. Not the car, not the *bure*, not the money that was wired to her.

"Has she claimed the plane tickets yet?"

"No, sir. From what I can ascertain, Brian has helped her make her own arrangements for her return trip. It seems she's determined not to avail herself of your assistance"

I can't say that I'm entirely surprised. Kennedy is strong and stubborn and she's had to let me go before. This time should be easy for her. And although I don't want her to hurt, especially not over me, it still feels like I'm being stabbed in the chest over and over and over.

"Keep an eye on her, Karesh. You watch her get on the plane. You watch her make her connection in Los Angeles. And you watch her unlock the door to her townhouse. I want to know she's taken care of the entire way and I want to know when she's home safe."

"You know, sir, that you could go with her. I'm perfectly capable of managing the rest of this cruise in your absence."

"I know you are, Karesh, but she doesn't want me following her. She needs space. Besides, there are some things I need to do."

"As you wish, sir."

At just after 9:00 PM, my phone rings. I'm still knee deep in contracts and accounting ledgers, just like I've been all day. My mood is testy to say the least and I'm really in no mood to deal with anyone. Unless it's Kennedy, of course. Knocking at my door, telling me that she's changed her mind and that she'll never leave me. But it's not. When Mr.

Bingham identifies himself, I'm both disappointed and irritated.

"What is it, Mr. Bingham?" I ask sharply.

"I have located the heir that was in question. Mary Elizabeth Spencer."

I sit up, aggravated but interested. "And?"

"It turns out she is deceased, sir."

"Deceased? When?"

Mr. Bingham clears his throat. "Thirteen years ago, sir."

"How was she tied to our family? I mean, was she an ex-wife we never knew of? An illegitimate child?"

"It appears she was, in fact, an illegitimate child, sir."

"Do you know whose?"

"I do."

There's a long pause during which I have to bite my tongue and keep a firm hold on my temper. "Well? Are you going to tell me who?"

"She was yours, sir."

I stand so fast my desk, which is bolted to the cabin floor, creaks. "What?"

My mind races back through all the women I've slept with, wondering who I might've accidentally impregnated. But I'm always so careful. I always have been.

But then, like the first domino in a long line, one telling puzzle piece falls into place and kicks all the others over.

My world is shaken.

Thirteen years ago.
"Who was the mother?" I ask, my heart racing.
"Kennedy Moore, sir."

CHAPTER THIRTY-SIX

KENNEDY

It's cold upon my return to Chicago. My fingers shiver as I turn my house key in the knob. It's not the eighty-two degree outdoor temperature, of course. It's the internal hypothermia that has settled into my soul, a bone-deep chill that I just can't shake.

When I push open my front door, a legal-sized, manila envelope is on the tile in the foyer. In what feels like slow motion, I scoot it out of the way to roll my suitcase inside. Someone must've squeezed the package under the weather stripping. With my last bit of energy, I reach for it to check the name and address on it. I don't recognize it, so I toss it on the counter to open later, once I'm unpacked. Once I can think a little better. Once I can move with less effort.

I wheel my case into my bedroom and park it at the foot of the bed. Exhausted, I perch on the end of the mattress. Every step I've taken away from Reese has felt like I've walked a mile. Every breath I take seems to be almost more energy than I can expend. The minutes crawl by like lifetimes and each lifetime stretches out into a succession of long, arduous moments of pure misery.

I take a deep breath and exhale slowly, closing my eyes. In the blackness behind them, in the split second that my mind isn't otherwise occupied, my thoughts return to Reese, as they have every few minutes since the agonizing one when I left him on the ship two days ago.

Hours pass before I even move off the bed, and more still before I make my way into the kitchen to feed Bozey. As I scrape food from a can into his bowl, I notice the lightly bronze hands at work. My hands. I'm reminded of my time in the sun. My time with Reese.

I manage to get Bozey's food on his mat before I wilt into the floor, before I let go once more the tears that seem to have no end.

CHAPTER THIRTY-SEVEN

REESE

I grit my teeth and suppress a growl of frustration as I get transferred to yet another useless imbecile at the offshore bank that I use. I wish for the millionth time that there were more hours in the day, and more minutes in the hours. I need time. I need more of it and I need it to move faster. The faster I can get things done, the faster I can get to Kennedy.

Since I watched her being ferried away from my boat four days ago, an urgency has been building inside me. I work tirelessly toward my goal, but still the urgency builds. With every day it escalates, it escalates to...here. Here, where I can't move any faster. Here, where I can't make *others* move any faster. But I have to try. Because I have to get to

Kennedy. I have to get to Kennedy, but I have to get this done first. I can't go to her with anything less.

CHAPTER THIRTY-EIGHT

KENNEDY

Hours have passed. Days have passed. Clive has come to check on me. He must've seen me return a few days ago. I'm not surprised. He's always pressed up against his front window, watching the goings on of his neighbors.

More than once, he has kindly offered an ear, and then a shoulder once he got a good look at my ravaged face. I've declined both offers, telling him that I'm just tired and that I need some time alone.

By the sixth day—six excruciatingly long, empty days since I left Reese—I'm not sure I'll recover this time. The love that a twenty-nine year old woman feels is far, far different than that of a fifteen year old girl. I have no doubt that I loved Reese even then, all those years ago, but I know it paled in comparison to what I feel for him now. I've loved him and hated him with equal measure. Why can't I just *not care*?

Day and night have lost their meaning. I'm up all hours and sleep in short bursts. The shades are always drawn to keep the harsh world *out* and me *in*. So when the bell rings, I don't realize it's the middle of the night until I answer the door and see the pitch black surrounding Reese's beautiful face.

My heart finds a hole in the floor and drops completely out of sight. While I wish I could hate him for all that he's done to me, I thrill at the tingle that I get from his closeness. It's as though all my cells are excited by the presence of his, the way water is excited by heat.

I say nothing. I just stand and stare at him. I could stand and stare at him for the rest of my life and never get tired.

He says nothing either, just lets his eyes rove over my face. Finally, he moves, but only one hand, which he raises to brush over my cheek.

"You've been crying," he says softly.

"Yes," I answer flatly.

"Over me."

"Yes." There's no sense denying it.

His eyes glow with profound sadness that even I can see. "I'd rather die than hurt you."

"Then why did you?"

"Because I'm an ass, Kennedy. Because I'm a driven, selfish ass just like my father. But mostly because I was completely unprepared. For this. For *you.*" Reese takes a step toward me. Slow, tentative, like he's afraid I'll spook. "I didn't see you coming, Kennedy. I didn't see you coming fourteen years ago and I didn't see you coming two months ago. I let things get in the way last time, but I'm not about to make the same mistake twice."

"There's nothing you can do, Reese. I won't be the other woman. I can't do that. I worked too hard to find something worthy in myself to let you destroy it for money. I just...I just can't do that."

"And you shouldn't have to. You should be first. You *are* first. I just failed to see that I wasn't putting you first. But I do now. I see it and I need for you to know that you're the only thing that matters to me. I can't let you go. Not again. Not *ever* again. Not even if you tell me to leave. Not even if you beg me to walk away. I can't do it. You gave me something real in the woods that summer. You made me *feel.*

"I've made millions, I've dined with diplomats, I've had the very best of everything in life, but I've never felt happy, *really happy,* until you told me you'd work on my boat. And every moment since then has been the best of my existence. Until you walked away."

He pauses, staring down at me with those gorgeous blue-green eyes, turning my heart, my soul, my *world* upside down all over again.

"I'm *here* for *you,* Kennedy. I've come for you. Without anything else...just me...I'm laying *me...all of me...*at your feet and begging you to take it. Give me one more chance."

"Reese, I can't—"

He interrupts me before I can continue. "I broke it off with Claire. No amount of money or business connections or opportunities or investments or contracts are worth losing you. I gave it all up. For you. I sold the boats and the businesses, it's all gone. I sold yesterday, tomorrow and forever *for you*," he declares, no doubt referring to the names of his boats, Ieri, Domani and Sempre. "The only forever I want is with you. Nothing in my life means more to me than you. No money, no power, no possessions. I don't need any of that. I only need you. I. Only. Need. You."

"Wh-what?" I whisper, afraid I might've heard what I want to hear rather than what Reese is really saying.

"I got rid of it all. From the time you left, I spent thirty-one hours straight pouring over books and crunching numbers, talking with attorneys and preparing proposals. Making phone calls at all hours of the day and night. I couldn't wait. I couldn't wait to get rid of every empty thing that might stand in our way so that I could chase you down and prove that I'd do anything for you. Anything. Just say it and it's done. I don't want a life away from you. *You* are my life. I *want* you to be my life. And I want to be yours."

"But Reese, everything you've worked for …"

"Is hollow. It's just money. Worthless when compared to you. I've still got more than I could spend in a hundred lifetimes, but if that's a problem, then I'll throw it all away for you. I'll be destitute if that's what it takes. I need you to understand that there is nothing...*nothing*...in this world that's more important to me than you."

"I never asked you to do this, Reese. I didn't want you to give up everything for me."

"But can't you see that I'd do it without blinking an eye if I thought it would bring you back to me? I *did* do it. For you. I don't need the boats or the women or the distractions anymore. All that was filling a hole that only one person could ever fill, only one person *did* ever fill. And I wasn't about to hold onto that shitty life and lose the only one I've ever wanted—a life *with you*."

"Reese, you shouldn't have done that. Not for me."

"Fine, then I did it for me. I did it because those things don't make me a better person. You do. I did it because those things don't make me happy. You do. I did it because I was afraid that words alone couldn't show you that I'm in it for real this time, Kennedy. I'll chase you forever if I have to. I'll never give up on winning your heart. Just please tell me that it's not too broken to give away. Please tell me that I'm not too late. I worked as fast as I could."

"Reese, I don't know. It's all just...so...so...I can't think."

"I don't want you to think," he says, grasping my upper arms urgently. "I want you to feel. Feel how much I love you. Feel how desperate I am, standing here in your doorway in the middle of the night, jetlagged as hell, ready to drop to my knees and beg you if that's what it takes. Feel *me*, Kennedy," he says, taking my left hand and pressing it to his chest over his heart. "Feel *me*."

I *do* feel him. I feel his love and his sincerity and the way his heart is racing under my palm. I know it's an echo of the frantic rhythm of my own.

"Please," he whispers, leaning closer and closer until his lips are pressed to my forehead, my hand still pressed to his chest. "Please, Kennedy."

I feel the sting behind my eyes again and I know I can't stop the tears that well there then spill over to run down my cheeks.

"Okay," I say in a small, trembling voice.

Reese's chest falls under my fingertips, as though he was holding his breath. "Say it again," he croaks.

"Okay."

And then I'm crushed, crushed inside arms of steel, crushed beneath tender lips, crushed with a love that feels as steadfast and true as my own.

Reese leans back just enough to let me catch my breath. He cups my face, his thumbs stroking the tears from under my eyes.

"Please don't cry anymore, baby. Not for me."

"These are happy tears," I admit with a shaky smile.

"Then cry yourself to sleep on me," he says softly, bending to pick me up. "Let me hold you until there are no more tears."

Reese pulls me in tight against him and I wrap my arms around his neck, turning my face into the curve of his throat. I taste the salt of my happiness as it pours down my cheeks and wets his skin.

Reese carries me to the sofa. Minutes or hours or days later, I wake to find that I'm still curled in his arms. He's fallen asleep beneath me, upright on the couch, his fingers laced at my waist so that he won't accidentally let me go.

CHAPTER THIRTY-NINE

REESE

Each time I wake up, I glance down to make sure Kennedy is still with me. And she is. Curled up in my arms, sleeping like she hasn't slept in days. Which, if her last few days were anything like mine, she probably hasn't.

Maybe this means things are getting better. Maybe we can finally have what we should've had all those years ago.

As I close my eyes and drift back to sleep, my last thought is to wonder when she's going to tell me about the baby.

CHAPTER FORTY

KENNEDY

My mind wakes not to the ultimate peace and happiness that it should. No, it wakes to the knowledge that now the only person who hasn't come clean is *me*.

There's something I have to tell Reese, something that he has a right to know. My intentions were good in keeping it to myself all this time — I thought only of Reese and how it would affect him — but now I wonder if I made a huge mistake.

There's only one way to know for sure...

CHAPTER FORTY-ONE

REESE

I decided days ago that I'd wait for Kennedy to tell me about the baby. I don't understand why she wouldn't have told me already, but I have to give her the benefit of the doubt. So I'm going to give her time. Well, at least as long as I can before others start to find out.

I asked Bingham to keep the information to himself until I was back in the states. I probably have until tomorrow before he tells my father who Mary Elizabeth is. But I'm going to tell him first. I want him to hear it from me. And I want him to know that there's no reason for him to address it any further. Legally or otherwise. I *want* Kennedy to have half of Bellano. I would've wanted our daughter to have it *all*.

I tried to reach my father earlier, but he wouldn't take my call. So here I am, driving out under the guise of getting lunch to try again, but with no luck. It's when I pull up outside Kennedy's townhouse that I realize why he wouldn't take my call. He had plans of his own. His car is parked directly beside where mine was earlier.

I grab the bags of food from the passenger seat and I make my way to the door, cautioning myself to remain calm. That's hard to do when it comes to Kennedy, though. The thought of anyone...*anyone*...giving her grief makes my blood boil.

When I walk in the door, they're facing each other right inside the entryway. Kennedy is holding a manila envelope and her face is unnaturally pale.

Her eyes dart to me and I see them fill with a mixture of regret and fear and so much sadness that it makes my gut clench and my temper rise. Toward my father.

"What's going on? What the hell are you doing here?" I ask Henslow Spencer.

"Reese," he says, surprise evident in his tone and expression. "I was just...I was...we were..." My anger escalates as my father fumbles for some plausible explanation as to why he's here, as he fumbles for a lie. "I was just catching up with Kennedy." I see him glare at her as if daring her not to go along with his fabrication.

Kennedy casts her eyes down and squeezes them shut before she speaks. "No, you weren't. I'm not keeping this from him any longer," she says quietly.

My heart is pounding as Kennedy walks slowly to stand before me, her head bowed, her chin trembling. I know what she's going to tell me. I already know what is weighing so heavily on her right now. But *knowing* it and *hearing* it from her, listening to her say the words, finding out the truth from her lips...those are totally different things.

"What is it, beautiful?" I prompt her, setting down the bags of food, to lift her chin.

She swallows hard and it kills me a little to imagine what she must be going through right now, what she must be feeling.

"Reese, that time in the woods...all those years ago...I know you used protection, but something must've happened." She looks up into my face, her heart in her eyes, tears shivering on the edge of her bottom lids. "I got pregnant."

I don't have to feign the surge of emotion that rushes through me or the way my breath catches in my lungs. But it's for that reason, for the pain that I feel watching her relive it to tell me, that I admit to her that I already knew. I can't watch her do this. Not for me. Not when I can help ease her agony. "I know."

Confusion enters her eyes. "You know? How?"

"A few days ago, I got a call from Malcolm's lawyer telling me who Mary Elizabeth Spencer was.

She was named in the will, so he was trying to find her."

"Why didn't you say anything?" Guilt, not anger floods her expression.

"I knew you'd tell me when you were ready."

"Oh, God, Reese!" she cries, burying her face in her hands. I wrap my arms around her shoulders and pull her to me, wishing there was something I could do to help her, to take away her torment.

"Shhh, it's okay, baby. Please don't cry."

"I wish I'd told you sooner," she moans, sniffing back more tears.

"I knew you'd tell me when the time was right."

"Reese, I'm so sorry," she says, lifting her head to look into my eyes.

"Don't be. I just wish I'd been there for you. To see your belly grow with our baby. To hold her before she died," I confess, my own bitter remorse choking my throat.

"I wanted to tell you, but they wouldn't let me."

My pulse thunders to a stop before it starts back up twice as fast. "Who is 'they'? Kennedy, who wouldn't let you tell me?"

She turns to look at my father. "Your father and Hank made some kind of a deal for money. He agreed to pay Hank if Hank could keep the pregnancy quiet. That's why Hank pulled me out of school and kept me locked up in the groundskeeper's cottage. He wouldn't let me leave. He turned off the phones and hid the car keys at night. He was furious, I guess because someone else had gotten me pregnant and he couldn't play his games anymore. I think he wanted the baby to die right from the beginning. He barely let me eat and I got really sick. The two times that I tried to leave when I thought he was gone, he caught me and hit me until I couldn't stand up. After the second time, he wouldn't let me out of my room unless he was there. He kept me like that until I went in to labor, but it was too early.

"By the time we got to the hospital, they couldn't stop it. She was too tiny to make it, too weak to breathe on her own. She died two days after she was born." Kennedy bursts into sobs so deep, they sound like they're coming from somewhere in her soul rather than her physical body. "Your dad came to visit me. He told me that it would ruin your life to know about her, that if I loved you I would never tell a soul. So I didn't. I never told anyone. Because I loved you."

Over Kennedy's head, I glare at my father. I've never felt more hatred for another human being in my entire life. It burns in me like a hellish fire.

"How could you?" I growl.

"I did what I had to do for you, son. For your future. You wouldn't be where you are today if you'd stayed with her. She was tarnished goods."

Tarnished goods?

Ice. My heart pumps one sudden burst of icy cold blood through my veins before it bursts into flames. An inferno traveling through my body.

"What did you say?"

"You think I didn't keep an eye on you? You think I didn't know what you were doing? And who you were doing it with? I knew all about her. Her perverted father, too. I saw the way he looked at her, touched her when he thought no one was around. He couldn't stay away from her. That's how he found out about you. He was following her and saw you two in the woods. He was filth. I would never let something like that touch you, touch our family."

I see red.

I release Kennedy and I lunge at my father, grabbing him by the throat and throwing him against the wall, intent on choking the despicable life out of him, intent on watching existence drain right out of him. "You knew? You *knew* what he was doing to her and you did nothing? You did *nothing?*"

My father makes a sputtering sound, his face turning bright red, fading into a dusky purple the longer I cut off his air supply.

"You make me sick! You are every bit as much a monster as he was!" I shake him, slamming him harder up against the wall as he claws at my hand, trying to loosen my grip. "I hate you! I hate that I share your blood!" I squeeze harder.

"Reese! Reese no!" Kennedy cries, pulling at my arm. "Let him go! He's not worth it."

I hear her words, but I don't care. To me, taking his life is worth it. It's a service. I'm doing the world a favor by ending him.

"Reese, if you hurt him, we won't have a future. It'll ruin your life. Please don't hurt him. Please don't let him take anything else from me."

The pain in her voice penetrates the haze of my fury. I see the consciousness dwindling from my father's eyes and I know how close I am to killing him.

But I think of Kennedy.

Always Kennedy.

I release him and back away.

My father slides bonelessly to the floor, gasping for air and holding his beet-red throat.

"I swear to all that's holy, if you ever, *ever* come near her again, I'll kill you. I'll drop you where you stand and bury your body where no one will ever find it." He neither moves nor speaks. "Do you hear me?" I shout, bending to scream into his ear.

My father raises hate-filled eyes to glare into mine. We stare at one another for a few seconds and I see the instant that my sincerity sinks in. A wary light flickers in his cold eyes and I know that he realizes that I'm as serious as I've ever been about anything. I just pray that he's smart enough not to test me. Because he will lose. He will lose everything if he crosses me. I'd give my life for her, even if it means taking someone else's.

Finally, he nods.

"Now get out," I say, dragging him to his feet and throwing him toward the door. "Get out!"

I watch him open the door and stagger through it. It takes all my self-control not to kick his ass onto the walkway and make him bleed, but Kennedy asked me not to hurt him. So I won't. Instead, I shut the door, shut the door on my father and that part of my life.

I turn to gather Kennedy into my arms and I let her cry. My chest feels heavy. Crushed, like I've suffered a great trauma to it. I hurt for her, for all the things she's suffered, for all the time we've lost and for the baby that I never even got to see.

CHAPTER FORTY-TWO

KENNEDY

I never considered how much it might hurt me to have to tell Reese about Mary Elizabeth. Or how much it might hurt him to hear it. The look on his face when he finally turned to me after coming to blows with his horrible father was agonizing to see. However, it was just another reminder that, deep down, Reese is nothing like that man. Henslow Spencer might've steered Reese in one direction or another, but not even his evil manipulation could kill the wonderful soul that Reese was born with. It just delayed its appearance by a few years. In a way, that almost makes it sweeter. It certainly makes me thankful that I'm still around to see it. I wouldn't have missed *this* Reese for the world.

CHAPTER FORTY-THREE

REESE

Waking with Kennedy in my arms is the only solid, real thing that I feel when I open my eyes. I've always known that my father was a bastard, but I guess I never knew just *how much* of a bastard.

I feel overwhelmed by wrongs that need to be righted, by mistakes that need to be rectified, by apologies that need to be made. But how? How can I go back and fix things that happened so long ago?

Kennedy stirs against me. She's my first priority. Making things right with her. Making things right *for* her.

I turn onto my side, pulling her into the curve of my body and pressing my lips to one bare shoulder. "Good morning."

"Good morning," comes her hoarse reply. I can hear her smile, though. Gone are the tears. I just need to make sure they stay gone. After today...

"Can we talk?" I ask.

I feel her stiffen. "Of course."

"I know this might be hard for you, but I need to work all this out. Will you tell me about the baby?"

I feel as much as hear her sigh. "Oh, Reese, she was beautiful. For the hours that she lived, she was the sweetest baby in the world. She had your hair, dark and a little wavy. A head full of it from the moment she was born. Her little hands and feet were the most precious thing I've ever seen. And the way she fit in my arms when I got to hold her...even for those few minutes..."

I can feel her anguish. It's different than mine, but I feel it nonetheless.

"Where is she buried?"

"At Bellano," she sniffs. "Near the cottage. Hidden"

"Malcolm never knew?"

"*I* never told anyone. I can't be sure who Hank told. Malcolm found out about her somehow. He might've known where she was buried."

I hesitate to ask this of her, but I'll need her help if the grave is that hard to find. "Would you mind if we go visit her?"

She turns in my arms to look up into my face, her pale green eyes glassy with unshed tears. "No, I wouldn't mind at all."

The way she presses her lips to mine, like she'd rather kiss me than to take her very last breath, tells me that this will mean as much to her as it will to me.

It's when we get to the old groundskeeper's cottage that I begin to wonder if I might've been mistaken.

Kennedy gets quieter the closer we get to the place where she spent such difficult years. When I pull to a stop in the gravel drive that approaches the house from the rear, I hear her take a deep breath and let it out slowly.

"Does it still hurt you to see this place?"

She worries her lip as she thinks. "No, it doesn't hurt. I just think of how much Hank changed after Hillary died, how he went from a loving husband and a good foster dad to a man who would want to put his hands on a child. It turns my stomach."

I reach for her hand. "I'm so sorry that I never looked deep enough to see what you were going through." It makes my guts twist into knots just thinking of what he did to her, even more so when I think that he cost her the life of her baby, of *our* baby.

She laces her fingers through mine. "You weren't supposed to see. I didn't want you to see. Although I desperately wanted someone to save me, I loved you too much to let you carry that responsibility. That's why I hid it so well."

"But I would've done things differently. I would've—"

She leans over to put her finger across my lips, shushing me. "I know you would've. I didn't want you to stay because you had to or because I needed you to. I wanted you to stay because you *wanted* to."

"I did, you know. I wanted to stay. I was just so weak. My father knew all the right things to say to get me to go along with him. I just... I hate that I've let him go this far. I hate that I didn't put a stop to this long, long ago."

"But you're doing it now. Not all is lost, Reese. There is still so much life out there for you."

I bring her hand to my lips and turn it over, kissing the palm. "For us," I clarify.

She smiles. "For us," she agrees before she reaches for her door handle. "Come on. Let's go meet your daughter."

Kennedy leads me around the house and into the woods to the left. We walk along a barely-there path until it just stops, just disappears into the dense undergrowth. She strikes out to the left again, weaving through the trees and stepping over a hollow log until she comes to a little patch of yarrow that completely covers the ground. She doesn't have to tell me that we've arrived. The spot rests in sunshine and I can see the arrangement of rocks on the ground. They're shaped like angel wings.

Slowly, I walk to where the wings meet and I kneel. Instinctively, I know I'm directly over the final resting place of the daughter that I'll never get to see this side of heaven.

I feel Kennedy as she drops to her knees beside me. I feel the pitter pat of her tears as they coat the back of our joined hands with warm salt water. I feel them on my left hand, too. Only those aren't Kennedy's tears. They're mine.

We stay like that for a long time, spending quiet time with our daughter, neither of us saying a word. It's when we're finally making our way back to the car that I find myself unable to hold back another thought.

"Do you ever think about having more children?"

From the corner of my eye, I see Kennedy look at me, but I keep my gaze trained forward. I don't want to influence her answer one way or the other.

"Of course. But you don't, do you?" she asks, a tinge of sadness in her voice.

"I didn't used to. I've never wanted to have a baby with anyone else. But with you it's different. I don't think I've ever stopped thinking somewhere in the back of my mind that maybe one day we'd be together." I stop, taking Kennedy's other hand and tugging her toward me so that I can put my arms around her. "When I got the vasectomy, I talked to the doctor about the possibility of having it reversed someday. How would you feel about that? Would you want to have another baby with me, Kennedy?"

"Oh, Reese," she says, tucking her head against my chest, but not before I see tears fill her eyes again. I feel a pang of guilt that I seem to make her cry so often.

"Don't cry, baby. I didn't mean to upset you."

I hear her sniff several times before she looks back up at me. "These aren't sad tears. These are my 'happy as hell' tears. There's a difference."

I smile at that. "Well, in that case…"

I bend my head to kiss her. Fire sparks between us quickly. With all the skeletons out of the way, it seems that we are closer. And the closer we are, the hotter that flames burn.

"I love you," she says when I finally release her. "Thank you for loving me even though I'm not rich and I didn't finish high school and I—"

"Wait, what?" I interrupt. "You didn't finish high school? How did you—"

"I got my GED. When Hank took me out óf school, I got too far behind to catch up, and after the baby died, I guess he saw me as soiled goods. He didn't try to touch me anymore, but he wasn't the least bit afraid of hitting me or kicking me if he felt like I needed it. So after he died, the first thing I did was go get my GED. That's where I met Gena Lamareau. She was the teacher, but she also owned a little dance studio in town. Once she found out that I wanted to dance, she started letting me come by and participate in her lessons for free. Those were my first steps toward leaving my past behind and becoming someone that I wanted to be, to have something that no one could take away from me."

As I stare into her eyes, eyes that seek no pity, I know for a fact that one of the first things I'll do when I move in to Bellano, just a few hundred yards away, is to burn down the groundskeeper's cottage.

Right after I give our daughter the kind of grave site she deserves.

For Kennedy's sake, I push back my anger in favor of something more constructive. I raise my hands to stroke her cheeks, soft as silk and twice as fine. "You are the strongest, most beautiful creature I've ever known. Every day you amaze me in some new way."

She shrugs, but her cheeks pinken with my compliment. "Life either crushes us or polishes us. I'm just glad that we both held up under the pressure, that we made it to here. To now. I wouldn't trade a million happy childhoods for ending up here with you. I have regrets and heartaches just like everybody else, but I can't let them define me. I choose to leave them in the past where they belong and only bring along the good things that matter. Like you. Our summer. The baby we made. Those are the only things worth saving."

"And you. You were worth saving. Then. Now. Forever."

I love the sound of that when I'm talking to Kennedy—*forever*.

It's time to focus on that, to put the deeds of my father and the ways that he influenced us behind me forever. Some things are unforgiveable. There's no point in wasting any more of my life trying to find a redeeming quality in my dad. It's time to move on, move on to the kind of life that I want for myself.

One *with* Kennedy.   With Kennedy and our happiness and our children.

And one *without* Henslow Spencer.

CHAPTER FORTY-FOUR

KENNEDY

I watch the familiar landscape whiz by. Reese is taking me to Bellano for the arrival of the furniture he ordered. He asked me to help him pick it out, and I know he wants me to live there with him, but today he seems particularly excited to make the short trip.

The furniture truck is already there when we arrive. Tanny is bundled in a thick sweater to keep her warm against the cold winter air that's gushing through the wide-open front doors as the movers haul in heavy bed frames and sturdy dressers.

I give her a hug and a kiss as I pass. Reese does the same. As always, Tanny strokes his cheek and smiles into his eyes. "My two favorite people," she says, turning her twinkling blue eyes to me.

"Is it ready?" he asks.

Her smile is angelic and happier than I think I've ever seen it. "It is."

"Is what ready?" I ask.

They look at each other and smile, but neither answers me. Reese simply takes my hand and says, "Come on. I'll show you."

We walk down the hall, discussing the new additions of art and rugs and knick knacks here and there. Reese didn't want to get rid of his uncle's things, so much as rearrange them or add to them. We both love all the antiques and history-rich pieces in the house. We both grew up seeing them and feeling like this was our "true" home, so neither of us wanted to change much.

It's when we get to the room that has always been Tanny's that Reese stops just outside the door.

"I ordered a few extra things for this room," he says, his lips hinting at a smile.

"For Tanny's room?"

"Errr, not really. Tanny is taking one of the big suites in the other wing."

"Then what's going in here?" I ask.

"Why don't you go see for yourself?" I see satisfied mischief in his eyes and it makes my stomach twitter in anticipation.

I push open the door and I can't stop the gasp that bubbles up in my throat any more than I can stop the wash of tears that fills my eyes.

Before me, Tanny's room is nowhere to be found. This room looks like it's ready for the arrival of a baby. The walls are painted a cheery yellow and the floors have been re-stained to look like warm honey. There are fluffy white rugs scattered about and a white crib sits at the bay window, flanked by two brand-new, padded rocking chairs.

"It's a nursery," I whisper, my heart fluttering in my chest. "Oh, Reese," I exclaim, turning into his always-waiting, open arms. He curls them around me, tucking me warmly and safely against his wide chest. "Just when I think I can't be any happier..."

"You might as well expect things like this. As long as I'm alive, I'll always want to make you happier."

"The only thing that could make this more perfect would be having some family here to share it with. I hate that Malcolm couldn't see this."

"I do, too. He would've approved one hundred percent. But at least we still have Tanny."

I turn shining eyes up to his. "I bet she was giddy with excitement, wasn't she?"

Reese grins. "Yeah, she was pretty damn happy."

"Why don't you go get her?"

I walk around the room, ooo-ing and ahh-ing over all the tiny details until Reese returns with Tanny. She stands in the doorway with shining eyes and looks around what used to be her room.

"Think you'll mind having a little one around here, Tanny?"

"I can't think of one single thing I'd love more."

"I was just telling Reese that everything is perfect. Just perfect. And we get to share it with you."

Tanny covers her trembling lips with one hand as she struggles to compose herself. After a few moments, she pulls something from behind her back. It's a wooden box, about the size of a shoe box, covered with beautiful carvings.

"This is for you," she says, handing it to me. "And for you, Harrison."

I raise the heavy lid and there, lying in the pale pink velvet interior, are the birth records for Mary Elizabeth that Hank had told me were lost. I take out the white paper with her tiny foot print on it and I stroke it, my thumb so large beside it, even through my blurry vision.

"Where did you find these?"

"After Hank died, I cleaned out the groundskeeper's cottage and found them hidden under a loose board in the floor."

I don't try to stop the tears that spill down my cheeks. "I named her after the only people that I've ever cared about. Mary for Malcolm's wife. He loved her so much. Elizabeth for you. You were like the mother that I never had. And Spencer. Because...she was. She'll always be."

Reese walks around behind me and wraps his arms across my chest, setting his chin on top of my head. Just showing me his love and support, letting me feel his presence.

"I'm sorry I never told you, Tanny."

She waves me off. "It was none of my business."

"It's not that I didn't want you to know. It's that I felt like I couldn't."

"Why?"

I turn my head to glance up at Reese. He nods, agreeing that we should tell Tanny the whole story. She's like family, even more so than *actual* family.

I'm calmer now as I revisit the events that took place all those years ago. I'm not surprised when Tanny cries. She cries for me and for Reese and for the baby that never had a chance to live and fight.

Tanny comes to fold her arms around us, giving us all the comfort that she's capable of. It's when she leans away that I suspect her tears run much deeper than just our story.

"You two have been through so much, but you finally have each other. You're finally healing and moving on from the past. That's why I want to tell you something. Because I know that you're strong together, stronger than your father, Harrison, and stronger than your past, Kennedy."

Reese still holds me as Tanny walks through the room, stroking the baby bed and the rockers, letting her fingers trail over the letters on the wall that spell "baby."

"I was just a few years older than you were when you met Harrison, Kennedy when I met him. I met a man who was just as handsome and dashing, just as charming. It didn't take me long to fall head over heels in love with him. But like most of the men in his family, he had a drive in him, an ambition that couldn't be stopped. Not for any*one* or any*thing*.

"I got pregnant and it wasn't until I told him about the baby that he told me he was set to marry a girl from better stock, one that could bring good blood into the family line. I was heartbroken, of course, but as long as I had my baby, I knew I'd be all right. It wasn't until I, too, gave birth that I got my last visit from Henslow Spencer."

I drown my gasp with a hand to cover my lips, but nothing drowns Reese's. I feel it as much as I hear it. He stiffens all around me, hugging me tighter to him.

"My father?"

With sad eyes, Tanny turns to us and nods. "Yes. Henslow Spencer, your father. The father of my son. That was when that I learned he could be as ruthless as he was charming. He gave me two choices that day in the hospital. I could either never see my baby again or I could see him Henslow's way.

"He'd filed papers declaring me an unfit mother and he'd put the full weight of the Spencer name behind it, which was considerable even back then. He had been granted full custody. He told me that if I ever wanted to see my baby again, that I must never tell anyone he was mine. He'd gotten me a job with Malcolm and Mary where I would work as a housekeeper so that I could see my son when he came to visit them. Henslow assured me that he would bring him here often. And he did. It was either that or never see my child again. And I knew I couldn't live with that. So I went along with him and, until today, I've never told another living soul that I'm the mother of his firstborn."

Reese has stopped breathing behind me. I can feel a light tremble in the arms that hold me and I know his world has just been rocked...again. Only this time with gentleness and love.

"I wanted you to know because I don't want you to go forward in your life not knowing that there has always been someone in this world who would give up everything she has for you. Who *did* give up everything she had for you."

Reese's arms fall slowly away from me and I feel his body heat recede as he moves around me toward Tanny. As I watch the scene unfold with fresh eyes, with *aware* eyes, I see for first time the shape of Tanny's eyes echoed in Reese's. I see the square set of her shoulders in the strong ones of her son. And I see the special light shining in her face for what it is—love. Maternal love. It's been there all along, watching quietly. Waiting. Steadfast and true, like a mother's love.

As Reese gently folds his strength around the frail form of his mother, I realize that our world has come full circle. That, for all the pain and suffering, for all the lies and deception, that everything is as it should be. That the journey doesn't dictate the end. *We* do. Our choices determine the shape and path of our life.

Reese's strength and goodness has led him here. Finally. Just like his mother's. And just like mine. We all defied the odds and did what needed doing for those we loved and, in the end, it all worked out. In the end, love won.

It always does.

And it always will.

I needed rescuing. Even when I thought I didn't, I still did. We all do in some way or another. And Reese was my Superman. He was my hero before he even knew it. And maybe I was his. Maybe I got to rescue him right back. Maybe we'll rescue each other every day of forever. And if we do, that's all right by me.

EPILOGUE

REESE

Like everyone else, I'm breathless as I watch my wife spin, her long, graceful body twirling like she's on a string. She's mesmerizing to behold. She was born to dance. And I was born to watch her.

Nearly a year ago, I gave her the news of my latest investment.

"Would you stop cleaning and look at me?" I asked in mock exasperation. "Babies don't have to have a completely sterile environment, you know."

She stopped scrubbing the rails of the crib and looked up at me, that ever-present twinkle in her eye, her hair mussed from her vigorous cleaning. "Why? You got something else you'd like me to do with my hands?" She held up her gloved hands and wiggled her fingers, her tongue tucked into one corner of her curved lips. For a second I actually forgot what it was that I was going to tell her.

I let my eyes run over her beautiful face, over the extended curve of her pregnant belly and I was reminded of the gift, the gift I'd gotten her for the birth of our baby. The gift of her last unfulfilled dream.

"Maybe I should just wait and tell you after they induce you tomorrow," I teased.

She tore off one glove and slapped me with it. "Don't you dare!"

She hopped up and came to plop down in my lap, like she'd done a million times as we sat in the rocker in the baby's room, imagining what it would be like to rock him to sleep there.

"Well, since you're gonna get all ugly about it..." I winked up at her and she grabbed my face and gave me a rough peck.

"Tell me or risk the consequences."

"Fine," I said with an exaggerated sigh. "I never told you what I planned to do with the money I made from the sale of my businesses."

"You mean other than shower me with things that I could never have a need of?"

"Yes, besides that."

"Then no, you didn't."

"Well, I had a friend who was open to the idea of an investor. You might've heard of him. Chance Altman." I watched Kennedy's eyes go wide and her mouth drop open into a perfectly round O. "I thought you might know the name. Well, he was pretty keen on the idea of having a partner, as well as having a troupe based in Chicago. I was

also able to give him the name of an extremely talented dancer that I happen to know. There was even an opening at the Steadman Theater that some charming and resourceful man was able to procure for the shows. Three nights a week, starting this summer."

After staring at me for at least sixty full seconds, Kennedy leaned her forehead against mine and I watched the tears — her "happy as hell" tears as she calls them —drip from the tip of her nose onto the front of my shirt.

"I didn't need anything else in life to be happy, to be complete, Reese."

"But I needed to give you this. I want to see you dance, beautiful. I want to see you dance until your dream isn't to dance anymore."

She lifted her head and gazed into my eyes with her big, teary green ones. "You are my dream. He is my dream," she said, touching her belly with one palm.

"But you're mine. And I know you've always wanted this. And I wanted you to have it."

That was followed by some pretty rigorous lovemaking, especially for a pregnant lady. It turned out to be a good idea, though, because she didn't have to be induced after that. Malcolm Harrison Spencer came along just fine on his own.

I can remember with absolute clarity the way it felt to hold him in my arms—my child, a part of me and a part of Kennedy, together in the most perfect baby I've ever seen. I didn't think many moments in life could compete with the moment that I stood across from her and watched her lips move when she said "I do" in the front of the church, but holding our son for the first time was right up there with it.

Every day since then has been just about as ideal as I could imagine life being. We've fed him together, bathed him together, watched him take his first steps and say his first words together. I wouldn't change a single second of it.

It's been ten months to the day since I witnessed the miracle of our son's birth. Now I get to witness another incredible event—the first day his mother got to dance the dance of her dreams, on a stage for the whole world to see.

The smile she's wearing as she twirls and bends takes my breath away. And the satisfaction I get from knowing that I helped put it there...priceless.

I'm living a life I never thought I'd have, happier than I ever thought I could be. My son is at home with my mother. My wife is on stage where she belongs. And my empire is being expanded for our children. I couldn't ask for one more thing out of life.

But if I could, I might ask for a little girl.

Just one more little girl.

THE END

Look for Sig's book next
ALL THE PRETTY SACRIFICES
April, 2014

Keep reading for the first chapter of the next
Wild Ones novel
SOME LIKE IT WILD
March 4, 2014

A FINAL WORD

A few times in life, I've found myself in a position of such love and gratitude that saying THANK YOU seems trite, like it's just not enough. That is the position that I find myself in now when it comes to you, my readers. You are the sole reason that my dream of being a writer has come true. I knew that it would be gratifying and wonderful to finally have a job that I loved so much, but I had no idea that it would be outweighed and outshined by the unimaginable pleasure that I get from hearing that you love my work, that it's touched you in some way or that your life seems a little bit better for having read it. So it is from the depths of my soul, from the very bottom of my heart that I say I simply cannot THANK YOU enough. I've added this note to all my stories with the link to a blog post that I really hope you'll take a minute to read. It is a true and sincere expression of my humble appreciation. I love each and every one of you and you'll never know what your many encouraging posts, comments and e-mails have meant to me.

http://mleightonbooks.blogspot.com/2011/06/when-thanks-is-not-enough.html

ABOUT THE AUTHOR

New York Times and **USA Today** Bestselling Author, M. Leighton, is a native of Ohio. She relocated to the warmer climates of the South, where she can be near the water all summer and miss the snow all winter. Possessed of an overactive imagination from early in her childhood, Michelle finally found an acceptable outlet for her fantastical visions: literary fiction. Having written over a dozen novels, these days Michelle enjoys letting her mind wander to more romantic settings with sexy Southern guys, much like the one she married and the ones you'll find in her latest books. When her thoughts aren't roaming in that direction, she'll be riding wild horses, skiing the slopes of Aspen or scuba diving with a hot rock star, all without leaving the cozy comfort of her office.

Other books by M. Leighton

All the Pretty Lies

Down to You
Up to Me
Everything for Us

The Wild Ones
Wild Child
Some Like It Wild (March 4, 2014)
There's Wild, Then There's You (June 3, 2014)

Fragile

Madly
Madly & the Jackal
Madly & Wolfhardt

Blood Like Poison: For the Love of a Vampire
Blood Like Poison: Destined for a Vampire
Blood Like Poison: To Kill an Angel

The Reaping
The Reckoning

Gravity
Caterpillar
Wiccan
Beginnings: An M. Leighton Anthology

WHERE TO FIND ME

Website: www.mleightonbooks.com
Facebook: M. Leighton, Author
Twitter: mleightonbooks
Goodreads: M. Leighton, Author

CONTACT ME

m.leighton.books@gmail.com

Some Like It Wild

How far will a good girl go for the bad boy she loves?

Laney Holt is a preacher's daughter. A good girl. Her only goal was to get married, have babies and live happily ever after, just like her parents. Only that didn't happen. With the betrayal of two people closest to her, Laney's dreams came crashing down. Now she's left with an empty space she doesn't know how to fill. Until she meets Jake Theopolis, a daredevil with a death wish who has heartbreaker written all over him.

Jake has no interest in thinking beyond the here and now. All he wants out of life is the next rush, the next "feel good" thing to keep his mind off the pain of his past. His latest rush? Showing Laney there's more to life than being a good girl—and that going bad can be so much fun. Her only concern now is how she can ever hope to satisfy the wild side of a boy like Jake. She's looking forward to trying. And so is Jake.

CHAPTER ONE

LANEY

Four years ago, Summer

"Come on, Laney. You gotta live a little. You'll be eighteen in a few weeks and then you'll be leaving for college. This is the last fair you'll ever attend as an adolescent. Don't you want this summer to be memorable?"

"Yes, but that does *not* include getting busted for drinking under age." My best friend, Tori, gives me that look that says I'm hopeless. "What?" I ask defensively. "Daddy would kill me."

"I thought preacher's kids were supposed to be wild as hell?"

"I can be wild," I tell her, avoiding her disbelieving blue eyes. "I just don't want to be wild *right now*."

"Then when? When are you gonna do something? *Anything?* You won't make it a single semester away at college if you don't learn some of this worldly stuff now, Laney."

I chew the inside of my lip. I *do* feel ill-prepared for college. But the thing is, I don't *want* to do wild things. All I've ever really wanted out of life is to find the perfect man to sweep me off my feet, get married, have a family and live happily ever after. And I don't have to get wild to achieve any of those things.

Looking at Tori's expression, however, makes me feel like some kind of freak for not wanting to break the rules. At least a little. But she doesn't understand my dreams. No one does, really. Except my mother. She was the same way when she was my age and she found everything she wanted in life when she met my father.

"Come on, Laney. Just this once."

"Why? What is the big deal about getting it here? Getting it now?"

"Because I want to get it *from him.*"

"Why?" I ask again. "What's the big deal?"

"I've had a crush on him for years, that's what the big deal is. He went off to college and I haven't seen him since. But now he's here. And I need a wing woman." When I don't immediately relent, she presses. "Pleeeeeease. For meeeeee."

I sigh. I have to give Tori credit for being one seriously gifted manipulator. It's a wonder I'm *not* wild as a buck. She talks me into doing things I don't want to do *all the time*. It's just that, so far, they've been fairly innocent. Being the preacher's daughter and living with such strict parents makes it hard for me to get into *too* much trouble. Tori ought to be happy about that. If it weren't for the restrictions being my friend has placed indirectly on her, she'd probably be a pregnant, drug-addicted criminal by now.

But she's not. Partly because of me and my "taming" influence. And it's those stark differences in our personalities that make us such good friends. We balance each other perfectly. She keeps me on my toes. I keep her out of Juvie.

"Fine," I growl. "Come on. But so help me, if he tells on us, I'm blaming you."

Tori squeals and bounces up and down, her ample boobs threatening to overcome the extremely low neckline of her shirt.

"Why don't you just go over and do that in front of him a couple of times? I'm sure he'd give you anything you want."

"That'll come later," Tori says, ruffling her blond bangs and waggling her eyebrows.

I roll my eyes as we start off across the fairgrounds. As we near the farm truck where the shirtless guy is unloading crates, I ask Tori again, "Now who did you say he is?"

"Jake Theopolis."

"Theopolis? As in the peach orchard Theopolises?"

"Yep, that's his family."

"Why don't I remember him?"

"Because your hormones slept through your freshman year. He was a senior. Jenna Theopolis's older brother."

"You know my father would've killed me if I'd been caught hanging around with Jenna Theopolis. She was pretty wild. That's about the only thing I knew about her. I'm sure that's why I don't remember her brother."

"How could you not? He was one of the hottest guys in school. Played baseball. Dated pretty much all the hot girls."

"Except for you," I add before she can.

She grins and elbows me in the ribs. "Except for me."

"And you're sure he won't try to get us into trouble?"

"I'm positive. He was a bad boy. I'm sure there's nothing we could think of that he hasn't done ten times over." We stop a few feet behind him and I hear Tori whisper, "Good God, look at him."

So I do.

I can see why Tori would find him appealing. His tanned skin is glistening in the hot Carolina sun. The well-defined muscles in his chest and shoulders ripple as he picks up a crate from the back of the truck, and his washboard abs contract as he swivels to set it on the ground. His worn blue jeans hang low on his narrow hips, giving us an almost-indecent look at the way the thin trail of hair that leads away from his navel disappears into the waistband.

But then Tori's words come back to me and I'm immediately turned off. She said he's a bad boy. And I'm not interested in bad boys. They don't figure into my plans. At all. In any way. That's why I don't have to worry about being attracted to him.

Even though he's hot as blazes.

Tori clears her throat as we move closer. "Hi, Jake."

Jake's dark head turns toward us as he pauses in his work to wipe his brow. He looks first at Tori. "Hi," he replies around the toothpick stuck in one corner of his mouth. His voice is low and hoarse. His smile is polite and I think to myself that he's handsome enough, but nothing to warrant Tori's insistence to talk to him.

But then he looks over *at me*.

Even with him squinting in the bright sun, his eyes steal my breath. Set in his tan face and framed by his black hair and black lashes, they're striking. The amber color is like honey, honey I feel all the way down in my stomach—warm and gooey.

"Hi," he says again, one side of his mouth curling up into a cocky grin.

For some reason, I can't think of one single thing to say. Not even a casual greeting, one that I would give a perfect stranger. I stare at him for several long seconds until, finally, he chuckles and turns back to Tori.

"What's wrong with her?"

"Uh, she's just shy."

"Shy?" he asks, turning his attention back to me. I almost wish he hadn't. My belly is still full of hot liquid and I'm starting to feel breathless. "Hmm, I don't meet shy girls very often."

From the corner of my eye, I see Tori wave her hand dismissively. "Eh, she'll loosen up in a minute. In fact, that's sort of why we're here."

Jake glances back to Tori, releasing me from the prison of his strange eyes. I take a slow, deep breath to settle my swimming head.

"Oh, I've gotta hear this," he says, leaning back against the tail gate and crossing his arms over his chest. I can't help but notice how his biceps bulge with the action.

Tori steps closer to him and whispers, "We were sort of hoping you'd sell us a bottle of that peach wine. You know, on the down low."

He looks from Tori to me and back again before he bends to pick up one bottle. "One of these? To loosen her up?"

"Yep. It's sure to do the trick."

His golden eyes return to me as he slowly straightens to his full height. "I don't believe you. I don't think she'll drink it." His gaze drops to my mouth and then on down my neck and chest, to my stomach and my bare legs. I wonder what he's seeing—just the light green strapless sundress that sets off my tan? Or is he imagining what's underneath? What's underneath my clothes? Underneath my skin? "I think she looks like a good girl. And good girls don't drink."

The fact that he so accurately pegged me stirs up my temper for some reason. Immediately defensive, I pull in my stomach, puff out my chest, and jack up my chin. "What? I'm just some simple, one-dimensional country girl? Is that it?"

He shrugs, his eyes never leaving mine. "Am I wrong?"

"Yes," I declare defiantly, even though it's an outright lie. "You couldn't be more wrong."

One raven brow shoots up in challenge. "Oh yeah? Prove it."

Too proud to back down, I reach out and snatch the bottle from his fingers, unscrew the lid and tip it back, taking one long gulp.

It's just local, homemade wine from his daddy's peach orchard, but that doesn't mean the alcohol doesn't sting the throat of someone who's not used to drinking.

As I lower the bottle and swallow what's left in my mouth, my eyes water with the effort not to sputter. Jake watches me until my cheeks are no longer full of the wine.

"Satisfied?" I ask, shoving the bottle into the center of his broad chest.

"I'll be damned," he says softly.

Ignoring the way his voice makes my stomach clench, I reach for Tori's hand. "Come on. We have to get back for our shift in the booth."

Tossing my hair, I turn and stomp off with as much dignity as I can muster. Tori is reluctant, but when I tug, she follows along.

"What the hell are you doing? You just totally screwed that up for me. Not to mention that you left the wine."

"We don't need that jerk's wine."

"Uh, yeah, we do. And what's this about the shift at the booth? We aren't supposed to be there for another forty minutes."

"Then we'll go early. It's just a kissing booth, for Pete's sake. It won't kill you to work another forty minutes. In fact, you'll probably like it."

"What's that supposed to mean?" she asks indignantly.

I pause in my mad trudging to look at her. I shake my head to clear it. I don't know how that Jake guy managed to get under my skin so quickly, but he did.

"Sorry, Tori. I didn't mean anything by it. I'm just aggravated."

"I can see that. But why? What did he ever do to you?"

"I don't know. Nothing, I suppose. I just hate it when people assume the worst about me."

"Assuming you're a good girl is not a bad thing."

"He sure made it seem like it was." I start walking again and look back at Tori until she catches up. "Besides, weren't you just fussing at me for not living a little?"

"Yes, but this is not really what I had in mind."

I smile and loop my arm through hers, hoping for a quick reconciliation so we can leave the topic of Jake behind. "Be careful what you ask for then, right?"

She sighs. "I guess."

"Now then, let's go."

****

Twenty minutes later, I'm regretting my rash decision. I've kissed the cheek of every pimple-faced boy in town. Tori has jumped in front of me to take all the cute guys that have come. Not that I have a problem with that. I guess I owe her since I messed up her meet with Jake. Besides, I'm not interested in any of the boys from Greenfield. The only reason I'm working the booth at all is to raise funds for the church.

I smile politely as I take two dollars from the next boy in line. He looks like he can't be a day over twelve. I bend forward to give his cheek a peck. I press my lips to it and then offer mine. He kisses it sweetly then looks shyly away. "Thank you for the kiss," I say for the hundredth time. I look down as I put the money in my till. When I glance up, prepared to ask for the next person in line, my heart stops and the words die on my tongue.

Standing in front of me, smiling like he knows I can't breathe, is Jake Theopolis. He's wearing a t-shirt now, a blue one that fits snugly over his wide shoulders. His pecs shift beneath the material as he digs in the front pocket of his jeans. I see him toss a ten dollar bill onto the counter in front of me. Confused, my eyes flicker back up to his. The bright, liquid orbs are intent on mine.

"I came for the peaches," he says quietly. He reaches up to take the toothpick from between his lips. I watch, spellbound, as his face gets closer and closer. "I need a taste before I go," he whispers, his sweet cinnamon breath fanning my lips.

And then his mouth is brushing mine. I don't even think to resist. In fact, I don't think at all. I only feel.

His lips are soft against mine and he smells like soap and clean sweat. His touch is feather light until he tilts his head to the side and deepens the kiss. I feel his tongue trace the crease of my lips until I part them to let him in. In long, leisurely strokes, his tongue licks at mine, like he's savoring the flavor of it. I savor him right back, drinking in the hint of cinnamon in his mouth. I lean toward him, bracing myself on the counter, afraid my legs won't hold me up much longer.

Finally, he leans back and looks down into my stunned face. "Mmm, that's the sweetest peach I've had in a long time," he purrs. When he winks at me, I feel a gush of heat pour into my stomach like hot lava.

Without another word, he turns and walks away.

COMING MARCH 4, 2014

8748300R00181

Printed in Great Britain
by Amazon.co.uk, Ltd.,
Marston Gate.